W9-DDU-508

For Vince & Terry
PAX Vobiscum
Xmas/17
from
Jim & Kathy

Requiem for Black Shoes

by

Ken Hills

Library and Archives Canada Cataloguing in Publication

Hills, Ken, 1938-
Requiem for Black Shoes / Ken Hills.

ISBN 978-0-9784032-5-6

I. Title.

PS8615.I425R46 2010 C813'.6 C2010-903149-0

Copyright 2010 by Ken Hills

And whoever receives one such little child for my sake, receives me. But whoever causes one of these little ones to sin, it were better for him to have a great millstone hung around his neck, and to be drowned in the depths of the sea." Matthew, 18, 5, 6

ACKNOWLEDGEMENTS

Where do I start? In this day of electronic wizardry, it really does take a computer savvy person to wade through the labyrinth of cyberspace. Anna Picco is my electronic tour guide. How many phone calls did I make and how frustrated she must have been with my naive questions! I could not have done this without Anna's help.

I certainly want to thank my family for their love and support over the years. You too were victims of my past.

I need to thank my psychiatrist, a woman, whom you will meet in my story. Her patience and guidance resulted in the enlightenment and understanding of my past and the reasons for my behavioural patterns. With that understanding came a calm of peaceful acceptance.

Of course, I want to thank my two main guardian angels in this life for their unconditional love and their support. My mother, a true bluenoser from Nova Scotia and my wife, Louise, from Newfoundland, have been the mainstays of my existence. What is it about those Maritimers?

My mom was an amateur entertainer. When she was 78 years of age, she was entertaining the veterans at Sunnybrook Hospital in Toronto. She had been doing that for years. She would play all the old war songs and sing with them and they loved her. How could you not? She told me at the time that when she became old, she would hope that someone would entertain her as well. She died shortly after but is with me every day.

I have been a rebuilding project for Louise from the first time we met. She always saw something in me that was worth redeeming and never gave up. Her love and support have been unconditional. Louise has also been my best friend, my proofreader and editor. She is excellent at all three.

Is it any wonder that I think of God as a woman? My sincere thanks to all of you and I hope you enjoy this book, the one you helped me to create.

Prologue

As members of the human race, we can share in the victories and the achievements of others. Because we share the same human condition and encounter problems along life's journey, we have the ability to empathize with our fellow man. We each have an intellect and we have emotion and often the two are in conflict with one another. That is why we are so alike in nature and can be influenced in both good and bad ways. I truly believe as the poet says that "I am part of all that I have met."

For thirty two years, I worked with teenagers, as a teacher, as an administrator and as a counsellor. It was in this latter position that I became most aware of and involved with troubled teenagers. One common denominator they shared was they came from dysfunctional homes. They were homes in which the parents were not present. Perhaps the parents were divorced or separated or possibly one had died. It could have been that both parents were absent at crucial times during the day because they had work commitments. It may have been a home in which the cultural views clashed with those more prevalent in North America. I personally knew of many young people who were abused either sexually, physically or emotionally. When that happens to anyone, the natural compass which we all have is disrupted and the youngster, who is already battling with the challenges of a normal development, now has to find his way through life as well as he can, carrying an extra burden. Some turn to drugs, others to alcohol. Virtually all of them seek the company of others who are experiencing similar difficulties.

I have written this narrative in the first person for a number of reasons. Having been sexually molested by a

Catholic priest, I can easily identify with the troubled teenager. Also, their story is really my story as much as it is yours. Through the support of my family and also with professional support, I have been able to lead what most would say is a normal life.

I was born a Catholic and I will die a Catholic. I am not nor have I ever been angry with the Catholic church. There are countless priests who lead exemplary lives by giving themselves to the service of God, the church and its people. I respect and admire them. Unfortunately, I was victimized by a bad person. What he did to me has not permanently affected my faith nor my relationship with a loving God. Certainly, there were times when I was angry at both. As I have come to learn, the divine Director can always convert a negative into a positive if we just let go and let God.

This book is for those children all over the world who have known abuse of any kind and have not been as fortunate as I. This is a factual story with fictional embellishments.

A friend of mine introduced this poem to me recently when he read it at a function we were both attending. He agreed to allow me to use it. It is written by the most famous poet of all - anonymous. I include it here because it has significance in the story which I am about to tell.

If you can start the day without caffeine
and can get going without pep pills,
if you can eat the same food every day and be grateful for it,
if you can resist complaining and boring people with your troubles,
if you can understand when your loved ones are too busy to give you any time,

if you can take criticism and blame without resentment,
if you can ignore a friend's limited education and never correct him
and resist treating a rich friend better than a poor friend,
if you can face the world without lies or deceit,
if you can conquer tension without medical help,
if you can relax without liquor
and sleep without the aid of drugs,
if you can say honestly that deep in your heart you have no prejudice against creed, colour, religion or politics,
Then, my friend, you are almost as good as your dog.

Here's to a better world!

Chapter One

"I see Fr. Whiskers was murdered yesterday. God knows the son of a bitch had it coming to him."

Chapter Two

Granny didn't even wince. She was good at that, her face registering neither pleasure nor pain. A stoic, I suppose most would say, but I bet she's had an ulcer or if she hasn't she will have. How can anyone listen to all these horror stories and not be affected by them? A bit of a thing she was like an Irish leprechaun. A ruddy complexion, fair hair, cut short, very little makeup and a very slight build. She did have great eyes, blue and penetrating, betraying an understanding and empathetic soul, eyes that were hard to ignore, eyes that kept you engaged and connected. Boy, did I need that right now. Every time I felt like I was falling or fading away, I would talk with her and she would reel me back in.

I guess I should really say that every time I spoke in her presence because she never really talked all that much. She would use all those conversational cues that shrinks use to draw you out. You know them. "Uh, uh, yes, I see, do you mean that...what you're telling me is..." Yeah, she was a great shrink, that Granny. Of course, that wasn't her real name but that's what I called her, mainly because she was kind, she was older and wiser and she was a woman, very maternal. Besides, I could never talk with a man this way. In fact, my whole life, I could never trust a man. I always preferred the company of women. And I don't mean that in a sexual way so don't try reading something into what I say. Any doctor I've ever seen has been a woman. They're easier to talk to and they listen. Male doctors don't listen, at least that's the way I always felt about it. It's the same with priests. I don't know why the church doesn't allow female priests. Just think about it. Women are by nature nurturing. They are in tune with their emotions. They don't try to suppress how they feel. If they need to cry, they'll cry. Men are too macho to admit they have emotional problems. They're always in denial and if you ever show your emotions around a man, then you're labelled a sissy. It was always that way with me, even when I was a kid. "Don't cry now, take it like a man!" When we were in the park playing ball or tackle football or just climbing trees, doing what kids do, if we hurt ourselves, we tried not to show it. Like they say in the song, big boys don't cry or something like that. Maybe it was big girls don't cry. Anyway, you know what I mean. Even when old Macduff in Macbeth learned of the news of the slaughter of his wife and his children, he was told, "you must dispute it as a man," to which he replied, "But first I must feel it as a man." Now Macduff, he was my kind of a man. He cried and he grieved and went with his emotions. When the grieving was over, then he thought about exacting his revenge. That part of Macduff I didn't really like because I don't believe in revenge. An eye for an eye, a tooth for a tooth. That is so Old Testament. I like to think that we have progressed a little since Moses walked the earth. But I know we haven't. It seems like the only difference today is that we have more improved ways of killing people and we can kill in greater numbers. Is it any wonder I get depressed thinking this way? But men have always been show offs.

Even the movies portrayed the men in a macho way. If old John Wayne was having a slug taken out of his ribs, he would just down three fingers of whiskey and bite into a dirty towel or something. Could you imagine Hedy Lamarr or Bette Davis doing that? Well, admittedly, Bette Davis is a bad example. She was always such an erratic character on the screen, she could probably have done anything.

What about Marilyn Monroe then? "Go ahead Marilyn, bite down on that towel while I take this slug out of your waist." I don't think so.

Of course, in today's movies everything is different, all because of the women's movement and I'm mostly in favour of that. There's the bionic woman, Xena the Warrior Princess and all kinds of female heroines. Honest to God, give me a woman any time over a man. When I say I am mostly in favour of the women's movement, I mean just look at what has happened over the years. Women, if they are working outside of the home should receive the same wages as men. No argument there. There's no limit now on how far a woman can go in the world. The United States even thought about electing a woman President. I never thought I'd see the day. Well, maybe it's time. Think about it. Oh, I know there have already been a few world leaders who have been Prime Ministers or heads of state. But there's not enough. What do you think it would be like if every country in the world was led by a woman? Certainly can't be any worse than it is right now.

But more sacrifice has to be made for the sake of the family. I mean if you get married today you have a better than even chance of divorcing or separating. What's wrong with that? Well, I'll tell you. If there were no children involved, it would be bad enough because any time a relationship ends, there are always hurt feelings. But when there are kids involved, it's a thousand times a thousand worse. If you are going to have a child, then take the responsibility seriously and provide for his emotional and physical needs. Too often at school, I have seen kids torn apart by the split of their parents. Kids should not be allowed to suffer because of the selfishness of two irresponsible adults. You know, if I let myself go, I could get really angry about this.

Anyway, I think Granny had a daughter of her own, no doubt smart beyond her years, like her mother and her doctor father. The thing is, though, she had her office in her house and the place was a mansion, at least by my standards. In a pretty ritzy part of the city, we would sit in her office with a window looking out on to a crescent. The street was lined with century old trees, a quiet cul de sac where old people walked small dogs. Old people like to have small dogs because they make the best pets. They can sit on your lap while you watch television and they can even sleep with you for God's sake.

Come to think of it, dogs make better friends than people, most of the time, even better than females. In fact, the best dog is a female dog. Male dogs can sniff out another dog in heat a mile away and then they do everything they can to get loose. Female dogs are not as aggressive as the male dogs and they become more dependent on their owners. Have you ever noticed how a female dog will take to a male person more than it will to a female? I have. I'm in tune with dogs and nature. I can fully understand why a female dog prefers a male owner. Let's face it. What's the first thing an owner does when they get a dog? Right. They have it neutered. Now the female dog has no chance of fulfilling its nature. So their best shot is probably a male owner. They can sense that, you know. What dogs do is natural. They have no hidden agendas like people do. And I think it is just natural for a female dog to take to a male person because they're just doing what comes naturally.

But dogs are very special to me. They will listen when you talk to them, kind of turn their heads and stare right at you. Sort of like Granny, I guess. They love you with no strings attached and they're always there by your side when you need them. I guess that's why I loved my dog and that's why I really miss her. I'd like to tell you more about dogs and why I think it's so important to have one in your life. They're way better than cats. Dogs ask for nothing. The only thing they really want is someone to love and to be loved in return. Dogs are good for kids to have especially because they teach young people about discipline, about responsibility, things that will help them the rest of their lives. We have always had dogs in our lives. Our kids used to take them to obedience school and train them. This always was a bonding experience, something that a young person never forgets. When one of our collies died, my oldest boy who trained her and had her in his life for twelve years, he played hookey that day and spent the next few days grieving. So, as sad as it is, even losing a dog prepares a person for losing other loved ones down the road.

My little dog, though, she was truly amazing. She was a Shih Tzu. We always had collies when the kids were with us. But when they left, my wife said that she wanted a little dog for herself. And the dog loved her but I think she loved me just a little bit more. My wife would agree with me on that one. I have these wonderful memories of taking the dog to an old folk's home. She loved it there and I would just ask the people if they would like to pat my dog and their eyes would light up and for a few brief moments, something special happened. Who knows? Maybe they were prompted to think of dogs they used to own or loves they had? Dogs can do that to a person.

I can still see her as a young pup. What energy she had! She would run around inside the house or outside in the backyard doing her figure eights and she could fly! She used to love chasing the squirrels and when one fell from a tree one day and landed beside her, both stopped, stared at one another and didn't know what to do next. The squirrel finally took off and my dog, in vain, resumed the chase.

Dogs are God's constant reminder of endless and unconditional love. They say that humans are made in the image and likeness of God. But I think that dogs are more like God and I'll tell you why. They both love unconditionally. They are as interchangeable as are their names. Dog backwards is God. Have you ever thought about that? Sometimes I think about weird things.

I always read signs and words backwards. I blame my grade three teacher for that. Ever since she told us in class one day that if you really wanted to expand your mind and improve your memory, you should do that. Another good way to improve your memory, she said, was to read off the numbers of a license plate on a car that goes by. If you're just sitting there on your verandah and a car goes by, just do that. Anyway, I'm obsessed with that kind of exercise. I've been doing it all my life. Watch this. On tfel nrut. On nrut no der tghil. You figure it out. Some of them turn out funny too. Our favourite donut shop is Mit Snotroh. The thing about the license plates though is now I have to memorize four of them and recite them to complete the exercise. Before we started getting so many letters on the plates, I would pretend I was playing cribbage and I would add up the score from a car plate as it whizzed by. Fifteen two and a run for three more. Five is an excellent score from a license plate.

In any case, our little dog had a few favourite treats. Cheese, peanut butter and ice cream. She would take these any day over meat, especially when she got older and lost a few teeth. As with all of my dogs, I couldn't be with her at the end. I just couldn't do it. The way that they look deep into your eyes. So, my wife was always the one to be with the dogs when they died. Another reason why women are the preferred gender. But when I knew the end was near, I did my best to comfort her. She died two weeks ago. She was sixteen years old and on her last day I fed her peanut butter and ice cream. Those were her favourite treats.

Anyway, I'm getting off track again. That happens to me a lot but Granny says there is a reason for that and if I keep coming to see her, I will find out what the reason is. I'll probably tell you more about dogs a little later.

"Why do you call him Fr. Whiskers?"

"We always called him that when we were kids. He never seemed to shave, always had stubble on his chin."

"I read about his murder but when you told me that he was murdered, you said it with such anger in your voice."

I started to boil again. You know whenever I got this way, I always thought about my dog and it would calm me, every time. I used to talk to her, just like I talk to God. But now, my dog's gone. I don't know what I'm going to do. Sometimes, I really do feel crazy, you know. I see this bastard in my mind hanging from a tree, with his tongue hanging out and his cross dangling from his neck. Boy, there's an image Granny would like to hear. "Didn't Jesus hang from a cross? Is he trying to tell me something?" But the truth is I never even told her about that image because I didn't want her reading something in to it.

God, I miss my dog. I used to love taking her for walks. The truth is she took me for a walk. We would get to the end of the driveway and she would look, first one way and

9

then the other and then decide which way we were going to go. Honest to God, why can't people be more like that? I mean size things up first. Take a good look at your options before deciding to do something. Anyway, my dog loved the kids. I would take her out when the kids were on their way to school and crowds of them would stop just to pat her. She especially seemed to like the little girls. She probably sensed that eventually these girls would be able to have their own kids, not like her, the victim of an unthinking and selfish owner. It was definitely a girl thing. That was the thing about my dog. She liked little girls and she liked older men, especially older men who wore black shoes. Honest to God! There's a reason for that too. She was first owned by a priest who wore black shoes all the time. I guess they all wear black shoes. And that really gets me too.

I went to a funeral home once to pay my respects to a priest who used to be one of my teachers. I don't even know why I went there. It wasn't like he was a friend or anything. Anyway, the thing I noticed right away about him was that he was lying there in his coffin, hands folded, clasping a rosary. That's not too unusual as anyone would be expecting to see a priest clasping a rosary in his coffin. What I really couldn't help thinking about was his black shoes. Do you think it's possible that he was still wearing them? I couldn't think of a priest without black shoes. Crazy, eh? But to tell you the truth that really got me. Like, couldn't these guys ever relax? I mean where the hell was he going now that he needed his black shoes on? I mean you could see your face in them they were so shiny. But the really weird thing was that he was wearing a Timex watch. Honest to God! Not just a watch but a Timex watch. I know because I took a really good look at it and it was still running. Now there's a real paradox. I mean did these priests know something I didn't know? They used to tell me that after this life, there was no such thing as time, no fourth dimension, timelessness, nada. But maybe there's a secret society up there in Heaven somewhere. Like God has a Timex watch. Yeah right. Can't you just hear God? "Well, Father Jacob, welcome into My Kingdom. I see you took a lickin' but you kept on tickin.'"

I was kind of relieved to see that the priest was laid out so peculiar like and was wearing a watch and probably his black shoes because it gave me something to focus on when I went up to the casket. God, I hate looking at dead people. It's a lot better now at funerals because the church allows cremations. I guess they finally realized that if God could restore a person from dust and bones, he could probably do it from ashes too. The resurrection. How would you like to be in charge of that one? I don't even want to think about it. I'm a pretty good organizer but when I die, I sure hope God doesn't ask me to help with the resurrection. God knows He or She will need a lot of help. And really, when you think about it, if God asks me to do something, I'm hardly going to say, "well, I'd like to but I've got this splitting headache right now." You can't lie to God. In fact, even if you had a headache, He could just put His hand on your head and it would be gone, the headache that is.

Anyway, imagine God looking at all of these ashes or bones and trying to put everything back together again. All the King's horses and all the King's men couldn't put Humpty together again. But I have plenty of faith and I know God will do a great job. I just don't want to think about it, that's all. Anyway, funerals are way better now because they usually just have photographs of the deceased so you can think about them the way you remember them and you don't have to look at some stiff in a casket. I hope when I die I will be cremated. What's wrong with that anyway? It's your soul that lives on. I'm always cold anyway. I'd be like that guy in the poem Sam McGee from Tennessee who became annoyed when someone opened the door to the crematorium. He told them to shut the door because "Since I left Plumtree, down in Tennessee, it's the first time I've been warm."

I prefer animals to people and I'll tell you why. They know how to deal with one another and everything in nature has its place. Sometimes I think that's the way God intended it to be for mankind as well. But we're too stupid to look at nature and learn the lessons from it that God intended us to learn. For example, it's not just dogs but take a look at birds. In the bird kingdom, there are bullies like the bluejay, there are thieves like the crow, there are hunters like the hawk and the owl. There are extroverts and showoffs like the mockingbird and peaceful birds like the doves. In fact if you go through the bird kingdom, you would probably find all species that reflect our own mankind. Just look at the birds and see how they handle different situations. If someone hurts one of their own, the others gang up on it and make it pay. Two wild geese, in migration, will leave the formation to stay with an injured member. And they will take turns being at the front of the V. They're completely in tune with one another. See how thousands of birds can leave a forest grove at the same time and never bang into one another. They should be designing our roads for God's sake. Schools of fish are like that too. Anyway more about that later.

"Pardon?"

"Did it make you feel angry?"

"What?"

"When you heard about the priest being murdered? Did that make you feel angry?"

Sometimes I would look at Granny and, honest to God, I could see her dressed up in a shamrock with her leprechaun head. She had a mellow voice, though, never challenging, never authoritarian, always kind of soothing, you know. But funny, because sometimes when I thought about her, she reminded me so much of those little munchkins in The Wizard of Oz. Even when she spoke and I really didn't feel like answering her, her voice came out like one of those little people, like she had just finished swallowing a pint of helium gas. It made me laugh, you know, just to think about her in this way. I didn't have to think about her like that but it was kind of fun in a weird way. Granny Munchkin.

"Why are you smiling right now? Are you thinking about something pleasant?"

The thing about Granny Munchkin was that she noticed everything. It was like those penetrating blue eyes of hers saw right through you. I bet she knew what I was thinking. I think shrinks are like that. I think they're like criminal lawyers. They never ask a question unless they know the answer to it in the first place like a good lawyer. That is, like most intelligent criminal lawyers. Not like that lady lawyer who was trying to prosecute O. J. Remember her. And O. J.'s lawyer too. "If it doesn't fit, you must acquit." Boy, did she ever fall for that one!

"You've been around priests pretty well all of your life, haven't you?"

"Seems that way."

"In our sessions, for the following weeks, months or how ever long it takes, I would like you to feel free to talk

13

about anything. It could be about your childhood, your teenage years, your working life, your relationships, whatever you feel comfortable with. Use me as a sounding board. After today, think about what you would like to talk about and I'm sure that eventually, by externalizing your problems, you will come to an understanding of them and find solutions. Perhaps today, we can start by looking at your home life. What was it like for you at home, when you were growing up? I know you're a Catholic but did you have a strict religious upbringing?"

Boy, did that hit a nerve!

Chapter Three

I already told you I talk with God. There was a time when we weren't speaking. It's hard for God to speak with you if you have your back turned. I know I don't like talking with people who aren't facing me. You noticed I said talking with and not talking to. Most people say talking to. Think about it. Anyway, that happens sometimes in everyone's life. Sooner or later, you turn your back on someone you love. Any time I was hurt, I would dial Her number and she would answer. Sort of like Tevye from Fiddler on the Roof. I could be anywhere, in bed, riding my bike, swimming. It didn't matter. My whole life I've been talking with God. I talked with Her today on my way down here in my car. I was asking Her about all the people I was passing along the way, the ones driving their cars, sitting on verandahs, maybe still in bed, maybe in a hospital. There are just so many people. I wondered how many of them were screwed up just like me. I'm betting there were plenty. Anyway, I always talked with God. Sometimes I would just say, God give me the strength or the courage. Sometimes I would just thank Her for all Her gifts.

I prefer to think of God as a female. I've already told you why I prefer the feminine gender. Sometimes I would be really pissed off and question Her motives. Like the time when my father died. I was only five and I didn't understand why he died. Someone said that it was his time to go and that God wanted him. Well, I wanted him too. Millions of people died. Didn't God have enough people up there? That was the first time I remember my mom saying that God never closes a door without opening a window. It was one of her favourite sayings. I didn't understand it then but the way she said it, with such conviction, it made me believe in it too.

Mea Culpa! Mea culpa! Mea maxima culpa! That pretty well sums up my life. I will take the blame for anything because I always feel so damn guilty.

"Confiteor Deo omnipotenti, beatae Mariae semper Virgini, beato Michaeli Archangelo, beato Joanni Baptistae, Apostolis Petro et Paulo."

"No, no no, William. It's "sanctis Apostolis Petro et Paulo. To the holy apostles. Don't forget the sanctis. When are you going to get it right? I want you to go home now and don't come back until you have the whole Confiteor memorized and memorized properly. Do you understand me?"

Father Murray, to me anyway, was really big. He had big feet, at least his black shoes were really big. I actually never really saw his feet. I don't think priests were allowed to show their feet. I mean I don't know for sure that priests weren't allowed to show their feet. Well, that's not completely true. On Holy Thursday, the priest allows someone from the congregation to wash his feet. This commemorates the woman who washed the feet of Jesus. It's just that I, personally, never saw a priest's foot before. I mean I don't know why this is. After all, Jesus wore sandals. I don't know why priests would never wear sandals instead of black shoes all the time. But they're sort of like nuns. I used to think "do nuns have hair?" Father Murray had big hands too. He even had a big head. Come to think of it, so did Sister St. Bernard.

She was our grade school principal. She had a loose tooth. Maybe it was a partial plate or something but every time she got angry, her face would get red and she would explode in a loud voice and almost always this big tooth would come flying out. Anyway, like all nuns, her head just seemed big because of that headdress they all wore. God, they must have been hot under there. Come to think of it, I wonder if they ever wore anything under those habits. That would be a hoot. I've just added another deep philosophical question to the curiosity bag. Like the Scots, do they wear anything under their kilts?

Anyway, Fr. Murray's head was just naturally big. And when he spoke, everybody listened, even the grownups. It could never be any other way. My mom always told me that the priest was God's representative here on earth. And I believed her, just like I believed everything my mother said. I mean she was my mother after all. So when I told her that Father Murray told me not to come back to the church until I memorized the Confiteor, she made me sit down at the dining room table and write it out and then say it to her. And I did it. Actually, I had a pretty good memory. I think reading signs backwards and memorizing license plates was working. Anyway, I learned it properly. And I went back to the church and I said it right for Father Murray and I became an altar boy. I was a pretty good one too.

I used to consider it a very special privilege, you know, being up there on the altar at Sunday mass, right next to the priest with his beautiful robes and his shiny black shoes. God's representative here on earth. It was like I was training to be God's representative on earth. What a privilege, especially at High Mass. You got to carry the incense. What an overpowering smell that was!

My favourite part of the mass, though, was when I got to ring the bells. Old Mrs. Mason, God rest her soul, that's an expression my mom used to use all the time, old Mrs. Mason always sat right at the front in the first pew and she would nod off right in front of Fr. Murray when he was giving his sermon for God's sake. I could understand why anyone would nod off when Fr. Murray spoke. He was always so boring. In fact, I remember yawning once when he was speaking and he saw me. Boy, did he ever give me hell for that! But I don't know what he expected. He was pretty forgetful, especially when he got older, like the time he wished everyone Happy Easter at Midnight Mass, Christmas eve. He was probably thinking about the resurrection or something. Who knows what priests think about when they're up there on the altar? When Father Whiskers was on the altar, I wondered if he ever thought about sports. I mean he was really athletic, you know. He probably thought about the altar boys, that son of a bitch. Anyway, I really don't want to think about that now.

Anyway, when I got to ring the bells, I would always look at Mrs. Mason and see her jarred back into life. The bells for Mrs. Mason were like a defibrillator. That was a riot. I mean why did she come in the first place? I think God would understand if an old person was too tired and couldn't stay awake in mass. I think She would be okay with that. It wasn't as if she was sitting around the table at the Last Supper, although that's what the mass is all about. I couldn't imagine being at the Last Supper and falling asleep. But if Jesus was right there with his sandals on, giving the sermon, nobody would be asleep, except maybe Mr. Mason. That would be Mrs. Mason's husband. He had narcolepsy. He even nodded off in the seventh game of a series between the Canadiens and the Leafs for God's sake. But then Jesus would probably have cured him right on the spot and he would stay awake, for sure.

Doc, I want to clear something up before I go on. Now I have always said He when I referred to God but now-a-days, there are many who would say She and even say that He or She is black or Asian or Arab or something like that. I like to think of God as being a woman, probably for the same reasons I've already told you. So I usually refer to God now as She. It's just easier for me to respect a woman. One thing I've noticed about women is that they don't prejudge you as often as men do. At least that's what I think. You may think differently but I think you'd be wrong. Women will listen to you first before they make up their minds. I sure hope that God is like that and that She gives me a chance to explain why I've done the things I have. Otherwise, I'm really in for it. It'd be the fires of hell for me for sure. I dread the loss of heaven and the fires of hell. That's another thing. Every once in a while, a phrase from one of our prayers that we learned as kids will pop into my mind. Sort of like something from Shakespeare comes to me out of the blue. Don't you just love cliches? Out of the blue. What the hell does that mean? Why not out of the red or the black?

Anyway, I sure am glad I don't have to sort out all the stuff that goes on in the world. Imagine how busy God must be. You think the courts are busy! I'm sure there's no comparison. Anyway I saw a sign on a car the other day that read, "God is coming and is She ever pissed!" I loved that sign. It sums up a lot of things for me. But I mean where does all this ever end? The women's movement. A mail man is a mail carrier now and a policeman is a police officer and a fireman is a fire fighter. Who the hell cares? And what difference does it make anyway? Are boats still she's? I love reading stickers on cars. Actually, do you want to really know what I enjoy doing more than that? I

19

already told you. Reading backwards. I can read whole sentences backwards. I can write backwards and spell backwards. I yllaer neam ti! I nac od gnihtyerve sdrawckab! I don't know when I started to do that but it is a habit I got in to at an early age. Maybe that's why I like dogs so much. You know, like God - dog. Oh, I guess I told you that too. You have to forgive me if I repeat myself sometimes, Doc. I'm older now and that's what happens to old people. I have friends who tell me the same joke, well, not every time I see them but often enough. It's just what old people do.

One of my old friends says that when we get old, we become like children again, in fact like babies. Think about it. We shrink in size, we shrivel up a bit. It's like we are getting ready to be born again. I don't mean that in the theological sense, although some people would say that. But young kids, if they tell you a story and you laugh, watch out. You're going to hear it again, maybe a hundred times, at least.

Anyway, my dog. My best friend demands nothing from me but loyalty and love. She's always willing to forgive me if I do something wrong like forget to feed her on time. She never asks me to do anything and gives me all her love and loyalty in return. I told you I had strange thoughts. Half of the time I don't know where my mind or my thoughts are going to lead me.

Anyway, back to the mass. I used to sing in the choir. My cousin used to sing in the choir too. He was a much better singer than I was. In fact, he was better in most things than I was. He was bigger and stronger, could punt a ball a mile and no one ever bullied him or me for that matter. If any bully ever came into our school yard, they had to go through my cousin first. This seldom happened but when it did, the bullies always took a beating and left cursing my cousin and vowing to get even. They never did. It was great having him for a cousin, almost like having my own body guard. Don't get me wrong. I could stick up for myself but I never had to. Even though my cousin and I used to fight all the time, if anyone ever picked on me, watch out. It was like he was the only one who could do that. He was my cousin but we were more like brothers.

God, I miss him. He died a few years ago. He was taking out the garbage and never came back in. He collapsed right there beside the garbage pail. But you know, he died the way he wanted to. I'm sure of it. But why couldn't he just have waited until I told him how much I loved him? I know, I know. Men aren't supposed to talk like that or think like that but I can't help it. He was a riot to be around too. He knew he was overweight, probably a hundred pounds overweight. I used to phone him and ask him how he was doing. He was always joking. I remember he said, "I'm getting a sunburn."

"What do you mean?" I said, "it's the middle of winter."

"Every time I open the goddamn fridge door and stick my head in, the light goes on." Then he would laugh. I miss him all right.

But I used to like singing at the funeral masses. No kidding. But those Latin funeral hymns could be pretty mournful. They were called Requiem masses. Requiem in pacem. May he rest in peace. Anyway, there was something about the Requiem mass that I really liked. Dies irae, dies illa, solvet saeclum in favilla, teste David cum Sibylla. Day of wrath, a day that the world will dissolve in ashes, as foretold by David and the Sibyl. Now there's a mouthful. That was the thing about the church when I was a kid. There was always someone threatening

21

you with mournful stuff, death and damnation. What a thing to sing at a funeral! You think that the loved ones in the church would like to hear something a little more uplifting than that. Now-a- days they sing uplifting hymns in church like On Eagle's Wings or Amazing Grace. The thing about Amazing Grace though is that it's the only recognizable song that's ever been played on the bag pipes. All the other songs played on the bag pipes sound the same to me.

I can't understand how some people actually like the bagpipes. I mean it sounds like someone torturing a cat for God's sake. Imagine being a Scot in the military and being spurned on into battle with the bagpipe. I mean just the sound of it would get me running if I was a soldier. I don't mean to offend those people who like the bagpipes. I mean it's a free world. Sorry, I mean country. I know how lucky we are. But you can like whatever you like. I just don't understand it, that's all.

Anyway, I wouldn't object if we'd sung those southern spirituals that you hear in the Baptist church. I would love to see the Catholic church rocking like that. It'll never happen, though. Some people say you can always tell a Catholic service because everyone is so serious looking. I mean I know the Last Supper is serious business but I bet God has a great sense of humour. Anyway when we are around the dinner table having dinner as a family that's when we tell jokes and laugh and enjoy ourselves.

"I told you I get off track. You have to be patient with me."

I don't know why I said that because if anybody had patience it was Granny.

The church was right next to our school and every day the nuns would march us down to the church for our daily visit. That's when somebody would cut one and everyone would start laughing. Old Sister St. Bernard, boy, she would get absolutely apoplectic. Like clockwork, out would come the tooth. One day I picked it up and gave it to her. I felt sorry for her. I'm sure she never farted. I used to think that nuns never did anything that was human. All they did was say the rosary and crack little kids over the knuckles with their rulers or give them the slugs with their leather straps. Anyway, if nuns ever did fart, it would have to be in their room where nobody else was. Boy, I bet if Sister St. Bernard farted in her room, it really smelled in there. I wonder if they took their habits off in their rooms. I don't want to think about it! But when someone farted in church, I used to bite my cheeks to stop from laughing and it always worked. Sometimes, I would make the inside of my mouth bleed because I was laughing so hard I would bite right into the inside of my cheek but it always got better.

The priest's word was always the law in our house. If Fr. Murray ever came over for a visit, we knew mom had ulterior motives, probably because we had been misbehaving like the times we played hookey and were caught. There were other times too but I don't really want to go in to them right now. Anyway, I guess I couldn't blame my mom for asking the priest to come to speak with us since my dad died when I was young and she had to raise a very active boy and three girls who weren't much older all by herself.

That was the thing when my dad died. My sister just came up to my room and said "dad's dead. Get up!" I was only five when he died. I didn't cry right away. Even though he was laid out in the parlour, that's what we called the living room back then, and I had to kneel and pray for him and kiss him goodnight and it felt like kissing cold stone, I didn't cry. But when the car came to pick us up for his funeral I cried, mainly because my mom cried and so did my sisters. But there was Fr. Murray or someone just like him at the grave side, a towering figure standing in front of the sun as I looked up at him. He was saying prayers. He had on his priestly garb. I thought, poor Fr. Murray, he's got dirt on his black shiny shoes. He's going to give them a good shine tonight.

But when the priest came to our house, his shoes were always shiny. It seems I was always looking at those black shoes. When it was time for him to go, I was always the one who had to ask for his blessing. And we would all kneel and he would make the sign of the cross with his hands and I would stare at his black shoes. In nomine Patris et Filii et Spiritus Sancti, Amen. The son of a bitch when I think back on it. Why did we have to kneel before him anyway? I know mom would turn over in her grave if she heard me talking like this but I can't help it. Those guys were nothing but guilt trippers. Mea maxima culpa - through my most grievous fault for God's sake. Boy could they make you feel guilty.

And the thing is we used to be forced to go to confession every Saturday whether we had sins or not. That's what got me. I used to have to make things up for God's sake because I didn't know what to tell the priest.

"Bless me Father for I have sinned, it has been one week since my last confession, these are my sins. I lied twice, er, I mean three times this week. I got angry with my cousin because he was the one who started the fight with me and I got the blame. I took the Lord's name in vain twice, only because I was angry with my cousin. For these and all the sins of my past life, I am truly sorry." And then he would give me two decades of the rosary for saying something I never did anyway.

Boy, if I only knew then what I know now, I would have told the bastard where to go. Imagine, now you go and tell your sins to some guy whose worse than you are, some guy who's been diddling with some little kid, God forgive me, or getting off on what you're telling him. Yeah Father, I couldn't help thinking about her in that way. I lusted after her. The pervert. In nomine Patris et Filii and Spiritus sancti, Amen. Like that Macbeth guy, man, he felt so guilty after killing Duncan that he tried to pray but Amen stuck in his throat. At least, that's what he said. Mind you, I have never committed a murder but sometimes I feel that way too, you know. I want to pray to God but I can't seem to follow through with it. It's like I have a blockage all of a sudden.

I remember one time when I was a teenager, I was in a play. It was called The Marion Year Pageant and it was being directed by a priest who was in a wheel chair. Do you want to know what his name was? Honest to God, it was Lord. Father Lord. I'm not kidding. Isn't it funny how some people have names that really fit what they actually do? Like I knew this surgeon once whose name was Dr. Butcher. Boy, there's a guy I would rush to have operating on me. "Paging Dr. Butcher! Paging Dr. Butcher." Can you just see those patients jumping out of their beds and running toward the exits? They might as well just start playing the bagpipes. And how about Chip for a golfer or how about a Math teacher I had once? His name was Mr. Inch. Honest to God! We used to call him Mr. Ruler. How inventive! And Mrs. Kitchen and Miss Grubb, the Home Economics teachers. I'm not lying or making these names up, you know.

Well, anyway, this priest, Fr. Lord, he was directing the scene called the Battle of Lepanto. It was supposed to depict some war in the bible, the Christians against the infidels, and I was a Roman sentry guarding something. I don't remember what it was. But I had this spear made of wood but it was painted with a metallic paint to make it look real, and I would hold it up as the crowd pushed against all the sentries. And somebody leaned too hard and the spear cracked and he stared at me as if to say if you laugh or even smile you're dead meat. Mea culpa! So, just like when I was in church and someone farted, I bit my cheeks and got through it holding the spear together so it didn't fall. Boy, did he ever give it to me after but I don't know why. I wasn't the one who broke the damn thing. But that was Fr. Lord.

We used to go on retreats, you know, when we were teenagers. Retreats, you know, you'd go away for a few days to get closer to God and for three days you would listen to Fr. Lord or someone just like him talk about how the devil would tempt you and how if you were bad and you didn't repent you would go to hell for all eternity and the fires of hell would burn you, world without end, Amen. And the worst part of hell would be never being able to see God. So you better be good. That sounds like that Christmas song, "He knows when you've been bad or good so be good for goodness sake." Actually, when you think about it, there are a lot of similarities between God and his angels and Santa Claus and his elves. Anyway, if I get into that, I'll forget what I wanted to tell you. Oh yeah. Fr. Lord would say, "now I know you boys are changing into young adults. Your bodies are changing and you're probably starting to think about girls and maybe you even get erections now."

I didn't think I'd ever hear a priest say that word.

Then he said "but you have to fight it off because that's the devil tempting you and you have to leave yourself alone because that's a mortal sin and if you start doing *that* now, you will still be doing that when you're sixty two years old. Always be in the state of grace boys, don't let the devil catch you off guard. And if you fall, get up again. Go to confession, confess your sins and stay in the state of sanctifying grace."

I was always confused about these things when I was a kid. I don't know what it is about religion. I mean I always accepted what the priest said but some times I wondered about how religion, and the bible in particular, was used. For example, some people quote from the Old Testament when it suits them but everyone knows you can't take the Old Testament literally.

That was before Jesus came along and the rules changed. Now don't get me wrong. I love Jesus. He is my ultimate role model. Besides it wasn't Jesus who changed the rules, Doc. A lot of these church rules are man made. But, you know, in Jesus' case, he was made man by God. What that means to me is that he had the same human condition that everyone in the world has ever had. He was flesh and blood, emotions and intellect. He experienced the human conflict. Hell, there are some who would say that He even had feelings for the opposite sex. I mean if he was human and all. Why wouldn't he? Like Mary Magdalene, the prostitute. They say He really liked her. Well, of course, Jesus loved everybody. I mean He was the son of God and all. But some say He had a thing for Mary Magdalene. But the really neat thing about Jesus is that He was a man of forgiveness. Try your best all the time. That's all He wants. Like a coach would say to any of his players. "Just give me your best shot all the time and you can be proud of your effort." I prefer to think about Jesus in this way.

And another thing. I don't hate anybody, especially priests. And I really do think that it is unfair to paint them all with the same brush. I mean I knew this priest once who was truly amazing. He used to teach at one of the local schools and was so good to the kids and to everybody for that matter. People really appreciated him too. They would try to give him things like money because they wanted to show how much they liked him and appreciated him. They would give him a new coat for example. But it was no good doing any of that because every time you did, he would only end up giving everything you gave him to someone who needed it more. What a guy! He used to take kids in and give them a home and he never fooled around with any of them. I know that for a fact. But, unfortunately, after the scandals of child abuse involving priests and mostly young boys started to be made public, he was forced to stop all that. It's a real shame you know how a few bad apples can spoil it for the rest of the people. It's important that you know that I really believe that some of the priests are fantastic. I like and respect many of them but not all of them. Some of them are assholes, God forgive me.

My cousin went to this school where there were a lot of priests. No one ever really talked about any of the priests there who fooled around with the kids and I don't even know if they did. But they did talk about the ones who used to hit the kids with rulers and inflict psychological torture on the young boys. Like the time my cousin was sent to the vice principal because he was caught fighting. He wasn't really because some kid knocked the books out of his arms and he tossed the kid across the room. I already told you that if anyone ever fooled with him, it only happened once. Well, anyway, this priest spotted him in the act of retaliation and sent him to the office. Then Black Jack, that's what the kids used to call the vice-principal, he said to my cousin, "why are you here?"

And my cousin said, " Father So and So sent me down to see you because he said I was fighting."

"What do you mean? Were you or weren't you?"

"No Father, what happened was..." and before he could finish, Black Jack took two leather straps out of his drawer and said,

"I just got a new strap. Which one do you want?"

"What do you mean?"

"You heard me. Which one do you want?"

"Are you giving me a choice, Father?"

"Yes I am."

"Well, in that case I don't want either one of them."

My cousin, boy, he was my hero. That's for sure.

"You're a real smart aleck aren't you boy? I'll be right back. In the meantime, choose one."

Black Jack left the room, leaving my cousin to stare at those two straps for forty minutes while he went and ate his lunch. When he came back, he said, "what are you still doing here?"

Naturally, my cousin was still there. His mother and mine were sisters. We were taught to respect the priests. After all, they were God's representatives on earth. How many times did we hear that?

"You've missed enough class already. Get back to class."

Now what kind of punishment is that to inflict on a young fourteen year old boy? Anyway, my hero just looked at him and told him that the next time, he could damn well give him the slugs and get it over with and if he didn't like it, he could shove it. This was considered talking back to a priest and disrespecting him. When word got home to my aunt, he was sure to be in for it. Except the priests didn't know my aunt very well. She was the same as my mom. They practically looked like twins. You see, she listened to her son and she believed her son's story and went to the school the next day and barged into Black Jack's office and told him that he was lucky she wasn't filing charges and that was only because she had always been taught to respect priests but he was testing her faith. She would see to it that her son and her nephew, that's me, would never set foot in that school again.

That's another reason I miss my mom and my aunt so much. Oh, they both had a French Canadian temper all right but they always stood up for their kids.

But those fire and brimstone sermons. They used to scare the hell out of me. I always went away from them full of fear and vowing never to sin again. But that feeling would only last until my next temptation. Then when I sinned, according to the Catholic church, I would feel so guilty, I would go to confession and then I would feel great again. It was cyclical. That's pretty well how I rolled through life. I always pray to God to make sure that before I die that I am in the state of sanctifying grace. Then I will go straight to Her when I die. I'm betting on it. Why not? Who wouldn't?

My wife and I saw this hilarious play once, Sister Aloysius Explains It All To You or something like that. It was a great satire on how much influence the nuns had over the little kids in grade school. Boy there was something I really identified with. You know there was this nun, dressed in her black robe with her rosary beads hanging down from her waist and she would ask the kids these elementary questions right out of the Baltimore catechism. The Baltimore catechism. Man, if there ever was a book that defined my childhood, it was the Baltimore catechism. "Who made you? God made me. Why did God make you? He made me to love honour and obey Him in this world and in the next." And every time the kid answered correctly, Sister Aloysius would reach into her pocket and bring out a cookie and give it to him. Think about that one. First of all, you couldn't see her pocket because her robe was black but how hygienic is that? It was probably rolling around in there with other stuff like old holy cards or something like that. She probably even had an old Kleenex in there. Who knows about nuns and what they keep in their pockets? Then she would have a class with these illustrations of Limbo and these little babies floating around on some cloud somewhere like that's where they went if they weren't baptized.

But the funniest part of the play that really got me was when these old students of hers came back to see her. I mean these old students they were much older now. One was a divorced guy, another was gay, another was just floundering in life. She would ask them all questions and you should have seen them fidgeting and the guilt on their faces. They were still afraid of the nun, for God's sake, and they still could be made to feel guilty at the drop of a hat. Catholics, boy, they have a corner on the guilt market. I remember when we weren't allowed to eat meat on Friday and it was a sin if we did. Sometimes I would just forget, you know. Man, the guilt used to rip me apart. I couldn't wait to get to Saturday confession.

"Bless me Father for I have sinned, it's been one week since my last confession. I ate a wiener yesterday by mistake."

"Well son, just say a decade of the rosary for your penance."

Just think about all of those Catholics who ate wieners on Friday. Now do you really think God would take them aside after they die and give them hell, pardon the pun?

"You know you're not supposed to eat meat on Fridays, don't you, especially wieners. By the way, they weren't Schneider's were they?"

That would kill me if God ever said that. I like to think She would say that. I like to think She has a sense of humour. That freaks me out. The thing is, though, now the rules of the church have changed and it's okay to eat meat on Fridays. But the thing is I still feel guilty sometimes when I do. Anyway, you see how my mind wanders.

At the end of the play, Sister Aloysius says to this gay guy,

"You know what you're doing is wrong, don't you?"

"Yes Sister."

"Are you truly sorry for the life you are leading?"

"Yes Sister."

"When was the last time you went to confession?"

"Well Sister, as a matter of a fact, I went yesterday."

"And did you confess your sin of homosexuality?"

"Yes Sister."

"Did you tell the priest that you were sorry that you offended God?"

"Yes Sister."

"And did you say your penance?"

"Yes, Sister."

Then do you know what she did? Honest to God, she took out a gun and she shot the guy. I'm not lying. She shot and killed him right there. When asked why she did that, she said, "well now he's in the state of sanctifying grace and he's going straight to heaven. I saved his immortal soul."

I laughed so hard I almost wet my pants. My wife and I thoroughly enjoyed that play and we discussed it a lot too.

My wife, she's a lot more liberal in her thinking than I am. We always disagree on the homosexual issue. She is so Christian about everything. "They can't help the way they are . That's the way God made them and why should they be shut out of the church just because they are gay? They have no control over that."

The thing is I know she's right. It's just that I am a little uncomfortable around gay people. But you probably know the reason for that too.

Anyway, where was I? Oh yeah, heaven and hell. We used to get these sermons from the Priests, especially when we went on retreats. They literally scared the hell of out us, well, out of me anyway. I mean the message was be good or you will go to hell. You wouldn't want to go there because you will experience physical fire for all of eternity. Imagine your body burning for all of eternity. And the really worst part of your punishment is not that you are in constant agony but that you will never see God. You will be forever, for all eternity, cut off from Her.

Now, hell is for those people who constantly turn their backs on God and are in the state of mortal sin. Purgatory is a little more hopeful. Actually, it is a lot more hopeful. Souls go to purgatory for spiritual cleansing. That's why it's important for us to pray for the souls in purgatory.

They will get to see God and to be with Her for all eternity but first they have to endure the pain and anguish of being cut off from Her presence.

When I used to go to confession, the priest would give me penance, usually, three Hail Mary's or a decade of the rosary. I suppose time in purgatory is like penance. I could do time in purgatory because I have always been able to do my penance. I mean I really want to be with God eventually. That's my goal. But we Catholics, we're conditioned to do penance, you know. Anyway, our spiritual cleansing, both in the confessional and in purgatory is incomplete until we serve our penance.

To be in Heaven is to be in the presence of God forever. Heaven is a place of eternal peace, no more anguish or anxiety. It is a place where all of the questions we have ever wondered about here on earth will be answered. Things on earth that we did not understand we will now be able to understand. To my way of thinking, heaven has enough room for people of all races and all creeds, a place where all can live in harmony as we all worship the same God, no matter what other religions call Her. It is a place where we will be with our loved ones, those who have been the most important in our lives. I like to think that if you are in Heaven then you become an angel of God and that you are then assigned to look after those left behind. Sometimes, when I am alone and I am praying to my mom, her presence becomes very real to me and if I listen very hard and concentrate it's almost as if I can hear her voice. It's a very comforting feeling but that's why I believe in angels.

When my dad died, I was five. Shortly after he died, my older aunt's daughter's first husband was shot down during the war and lost in action. The grieving in my house was palpable. Every time I turned around, entered another room, there was someone crying. But it was much later, maybe during my teen years, when my mom told me that she would pray to my father for help. My mom had enormous faith and never went to sleep without first saying her rosary. This one night she prayed to my father to take care of her sister's daughter. Her bed began to shake and she saw a vision of my father at the end of the bed and he said, "don't worry babe, I'll take care of Minnie." My dad used to call my mom Babe. It was hard for me to think of my mom as a babe.

Anyway, two weeks later a young man knocked on my aunt's door. This young man had just returned from the war. He was a bomber pilot who was shot down over Germany and taken prisoner. He survived seventeen months in a P.O.W. camp. He was also a best friend of Minnie's daughter's first husband and he promised him that he would look up his friend's wife if he made it home alive. The two of them eventually married and raised five children. So you see, angels are busy. And it's just like my mom used to say how God never closes a door without opening a window.

How can anyone not believe in the existence of God? Agnostics are the doubting Thomases of the world and atheists are probably people who have never really experienced any kind of religious sensations or events.

What I liked the most about the Catholic church was the Latin mass. I guess a lot of people agreed with getting rid of the Latin because it was a dead language. Well, what does that mean anyway? If you really want to capture history and make it stand still, leave it alone. History changes as we produce more historians. They are all interested in putting a different twist on the past. Little by little, almost imperceptibly, well meaning historians can change the past. So, Latin is a good thing because the mass stays the same no matter where you go in the world. Now, the language in which you hear the mass will begin to change because everything that is alive has an evolutionary component. So, I say let's get back to one language for all people in the whole world.

Anyway, you know, I can't understand why some people argue about the existence of God. Look at it this way. Do you ever buy a Lottery ticket? Why? Because you think you might win big money. But the odds are fourteen million to one that you will win, right? Think about that, fourteen million to one. Put yourself in the baseball dome that holds fifty thousand people. Let's say they have a draw. Do you really think you're going to win? I mean look around you. Now multiply that by almost one hundred and thirty. Put yourself in a dome that has fourteen million people in it. Does that change your mind? No? Why? Because you say, someone's got to win. Right!

If there was a fourteen million to one shot that when you die, you will meet God and then you will be asked to answer for the kind of life you lead, are you really willing to say there's no God? I mean if you are willing to spend your hard earned money on lottery tickets when the odds are fourteen million to one, wouldn't you play it safe just in case there is a God? People are stupid some times. I really mean it.

But getting back to priests. The way I look at it is this. Priests are God's representatives here on earth and I really do believe that. But you know what? They're no more God's representative than I am or you are or anyone is. People are happier when they are nice to one another.

"You know, you're an intelligent man. Why do you talk the way you do? You remind me of someone."

I knew right away who Granny meant.

"Really?"

"Someone I read about in a book a long time ago."

"Yeah, I know, Holden Caulfield, right?"

The eternal teenager? He will never change. Holden and I have a lot in common all right. I identify with him. It's a case of arrested development. But why am I telling you that? And you and I both know the reason for that. I used to be just like him when I was a teenager. And now I don't always talk like him like I used to on account of I was a teacher and all. That's just like him, isn't it? He would often end sentences that way. But I still think like him and sometimes I still talk like him. It's not that I'm imitating him or anything like that. It's just that Holden experienced something traumatic in his life too and I really think that when that happens to any of us we look for a way to survive the best way we can. If that means ignoring realities for awhile, then that's what must be done. If it means living in another world that is so much more pleasant then that's what has to be done. If it means suppressing what happened to you, burying it so deep that you cover it over with other activities, situations, relationships, then that's what you have to do. Because it's all about survival, right Doc? I mean if I really dwelled on what happened to me, I couldn't stand it. I would probably jump off a bridge or something. When I say that I identify with Holden, I mean that I agree with him when he says that people are phony. He probably used the wrong word but I know what he means. Like, people disguise their true identities. You should know that. Everybody is suffering with something, whether it is emotional or physical. There's always something there. We just can't go around revealing our true selves all the time. What kind of world would that be anyway?

And kids, the way Holden looks at kids is right on. I hope my grandchildren never grow up, you know, lose their innocence, the fresh young way they look at the world with curiosity and wonder. I mean we have to grow up. I know that. They will face those pubescent crises of acne, periods, awkwardness, peer pressure, hormonal explosions, puppy love, parental defiance. They will get crushes on movie stars or rock stars or athletes. They will struggle like hell to find their own identity. But they will survive it all. I know that the human spirit is amazing as it takes on a life of its own when we, seemingly, lose control of our lives. But why do we have to lose our kidness? That's what I mean. Holden's one of my favourite fictional characters. But he's not really fictional, is he? There are tons of people like him, all over the world.

Agnus Dei, qui tollis peccata mundi, dona nobis pacem. Lamb of God who takes away the sins of the world, give us peace. I loved the Latin mass. The thing about Latin is that the language never changes. It's like the little kids I talked about. Yeah, you might say I had a strict Catholic upbringing, confession every Saturday, whether I needed to or not, Mass on Sunday morning and benediction in the evening. The priest's word was law unless my mom said differently, rosary every night at home, holy water font at the door so every time we went out, we would dip our finger into the font and bless ourselves, high mass once a month when the priest stunk up the church with the incense, singing in the choir, educated by the nuns who never spared the rod, hours spent at the church for the exposition, praying, praying, praying, no meat on Fridays, respect, respect, respect for the priests, for our elders, never speaking unless spoken to. But it was my church, you know what I mean? It was like family. Only I could make fun of it or some other Catholic could make fun of it. But if a non Catholic made fun of it, watch out. We wouldn't fight unless we had to but we stuck up for our church. I don't know why intelligent people in charge of our education ever allowed a Catholic school to be built right next to a Protestant school. What were they thinking about? Were they thinking they might be able to convert all of the Protestants? All they did was guarantee name calling and fights. We were kids. What did we know? They used to call us dogans or micks or fisheaters and at first those words hurt my feelings but actually, the truth is that after a while I kind of liked it when someone called me those names. It gave me an identity.

I was proud of being a Roman Catholic. It gave me a lineage that could be traced back two thousand years. It made me part of a history that was filled with serious confrontations, many of which are still carrying on today. When you think of it, on the other hand, it is pretty stupid to be fighting over religion. I really don't think that's what a loving God wants of us. But when you're a kid, you don't know any better. You're of the same religious tradition as St. Michael the Archangel who slew the devil. When you were confirmed, you became a soldier of Christ. Yeah, I loved being a Catholic, still do, although there were times when I turned my back on God. But I don't really want to talk about that now. Maybe later.

I had two boyhood friends, one a Jehovah's Witness and the other from a family of Salvation Army. Anyway, we always got along, even Doc Ballard, that's what we used to call the Jehovah witness guy, after a dog food commercial.

I don't feel like explaining that one to you. The only thing was though my mom didn't think it was such a good idea that I hang around with a J.W., especially given the way she felt about them. She was a French Canadian Roman Catholic to the core. The priest was God and so was his word. I remember one time a J.W. conned his way into our house and tried to put on a record that would tell us all about Jehovah and how we, especially Catholics, should mend our ways. Well, before you knew it, he was thrown out the front door and the record after him. He never bothered my mom again. You had to love her spirit.

But kids are different. I didn't see anything wrong with the J.W.'s when I was a kid. But I must admit I don't like them coming to my door. I mean God loves everybody if you give Her a chance. No one faith has squatter's rights in Heaven. And my Sally Ann friend? We used to get together and phone the Sally Ann and say things like, "do you save young girls? Well, save me one for Saturday night." Kids do stuff like that. It's harmless. Now in the same way we would call the drug store and say "do you have Prince Albert in a can?" That was a pipe tobacco. Then we would say "well you better let him out before he suffocates." The point is we used to make fun of everybody and everything when we were kids. We meant no harm. We were just kids having fun.

Anyway, one of the ways we used to make fun of the Catholic church was pig Latin. This was our own version of Latin on the streets, a way to be silly, to say things that we didn't want our parents to know. Etslay amscray eforbay the opscay. fterafay eway ancay eetsmay tay the arkpay. It was all in fun.

"Tell me about your dreams."

I knew it was just a matter of time before Granny got around to that one. Shrinks always want to know what you're dreaming about. Like the subconscious mind brings all the truth to the surface while you're dreaming. I'm sure they think the real you is there, more often than not though in a strange kind of form that only shrinks can interpret. How could I tell her that she was in my dream last night? Granny Munchkin and Holden Caulfield. Now there's a pair for you. I always write down my dreams when I wake up because I like to remember them, well, most of them anyway. Some I would just as soon forget.

Anyway, there was old Granny leading us up the yellow brick road, me and Holden. I had my arm around him. God, don't go reading anything into that. I look at Holden as a son, that's all. Anyway, there wasn't just one Granny, there were twelve of them. I thought at first they were like the seven dwarves because of their size and then I thought they're not dwarves, they're apostles, for God's sake and they were leading us to see the real Wizard of Oz, not like that fraudulent wizard in the movie, the one who was hiding behind a phony wall speaking into a microphone but a real Wizard. To tell you the truth, Holden and I were both kind of excited about it. We were hopping along behind the Munchkin bunch and I didn't even feel any kind of chest discomfort. I have a bit of a ticker problem, you know, nothing too serious but sometimes I get a little winded, not much, just enough to piss me off because I used to be a pretty good athlete but that's another story. I suppose we were looking for the real wizard and he was hiding behind this wall in that great castle in the sky. You don't suppose that could have been God that we were seeking. I better leave that one up to the shrink. But, come to think of it, we were climbing up this yellow brick

41

road and going right through the clouds and the first thing I saw was my dog and when she saw me, she came running and started to do those figures of eight around me. She was so happy to see me, she couldn't stop running and jumping up on me. Honest to God, I would have been happy just to stay there and play with my dog. What a great dream that was! God, I miss my dog! Anyway I told her about the dream and she hardly changed her expression, aside from sort of smiling when I told her about the twelve granny munchkins. Truthfully? I really think she was flattered. But I've had other dreams too, you know. I'll get to them later.

"You know I'm going to ask you what happened, don't you."

I nodded.

"Not today though."

I was happy about that because, to tell you the truth, I didn't really want to think about it then.

"What I would like to know is why did you wait this long to come to see me? I mean you've been retired now for two years."

"You probably won't believe this but I hardly ever thought about it until a year after I retired. I don't really know how it came about, slowly I guess. I know I had more time to think about my life, about my family and my relationships with others. I was always the one who was soft spoken, quiet, observing. Now that's pretty amazing, isn't it? I mean it happened when I was twelve years old for God's sake and I never really thought about it until after I retired! I don't blame you if you don't believe me. I mean I thought about it right up until I was twenty one years old and my actions were those of one who had experienced something awful."

"Looking back on it, tell me how you think you changed after it happened? And then you can tell me about your teaching career."

"Wow! Two loaded questions. Well here goes, I'll give it my best shot."

Chapter Four

"Could I talk about my earlier days first?"

"That would be fine."

That's the thing about Granny, she would let you say anything. That's what I really like about her but sooner or later I knew that she would uncover the truth. I thought of her more like an archaeologist. She would just keep digging and digging until she got to the core of my problem and then, hopefully, she would show me how to reconstruct something that had gone terribly wrong.

But before I get in to my childhood, why do you ask me if I knew if any of my friends were abused like me? Yes, I know a child abuser never stops with just one victim. That's occurred to me a few times over the last year or so. In fact, I've been in touch with some of my old friends. Is that what you were getting at? Anyway, I was pretty certain about this one person in particular. That was my friend, Jack. He was a great athlete. In fact, he was the kind of guy you would think could do anything well that he ever wanted to try. The reason I suspect he was abused also is because of the circumstances - same room, same struggling noises, same situation. The thing is today that same person is an alcoholic and has clinical depression. How did that ever happen? When he was a kid and we played on the same ball team, he was easily the most moral person I knew. He had such a strong faith and in fact eventually went to study in the priesthood. He spent five years of his life in the seminary. Now he went from that kind of person to one who never went to church. In fact, I once asked him about his religion, remembering how strong his beliefs used to be. You want to know what he said to me? He said "if you ever ask me about religion again, I 'll never talk to you again." Tell me he didn't have a bad experience somewhere along the line.

I don't know why he went in to the seminary if he had been abused too like me. Do you think he was just trying to escape, to be where he knew he wasn't going to be able to do much damage? Why did he leave then? It's all conjecture. I don't know for sure that he was abused anyway. Maybe he was. You think he was, don't you? You say that the clinical depression and the drinking point in that direction. Doc, how did I escape all that? Funny, you know, but I can still smell the bastard's after shave and I can still feel his whiskers. I really hate that bastard for what he did to me and to my friends.

Hate is a pretty strong word. How do I reconcile that with my belief in a God who preaches forgiveness? Mostly I want to forgive him. I want to say that he is just another human being whose compass was twisted. He shared in the same humanity as everyone else, struggled with his morals like everyone else. You know sometimes I think about him going to confession. I used to think that priests never had to go to confession, in the same way that I used to think that doctors never got sick. But now I know that priests can't hear their own confessions in the same way that doctors can't take care of themselves.

What would he have said to his confessor? "Bless me Father for I have sinned, I confess to you and to almighty God, it has been a month since my last confession, these are my sins. I buggered two kids this past month. I entertained impure thoughts about them and I committed the sin of self abuse thinking about them. For these and all the sins of my past life I am truly sorry." Imagine being on the other end of that confession. I mean what would the confessor say or even think? Priests are not allowed to

45

reveal what has been told to them in the confessional, sort of like a psychiatrist and the patient, I guess. Oh well, when you get right down to it, this is between God and him. I'm out of that part. And I should leave it like that. Still, I can't help thinking.

What kind of childhood did he have? Was he abused by someone he trusted? Don't they say that most child abusers have themselves been abused? I can tell you I have never done anything like that in case you're thinking that I did. I find the thought abhorrent. Maybe you don't believe me? Well, it's true and I didn't murder him either, the bastard. But I can't help thinking about him. Was there a deficiency somewhere in his life, something he wanted to have but was not able to have? Was he dominated as a young boy and does he now want to exercise power over someone else? Life is just too complicated for me. But I am sure that if anyone can figure out this mess, She can. We have to have faith. At least, that's what I think anyway. That's all that keeps me going.

But let's get back to this forgiveness thing. Do you think I should forgive him? Is what he has done to me and to others forgivable? Well, I guess if you're conservative you would tell me to string him up and let him fry, that is, if he were still alive. If you were a liberal, you would say, think about it, he's only human, humans make mistakes, everyone deserves another chance, although it's pretty well agreed upon now that pedophiles cannot be rehabilitated. So what is the solution? The law could take care of him. God could take care of him. Why do I need to get involved?

Let's see - the high road or the low road? I told you I have this love of Shakespeare and his plays, didn't I? Well, I do. I really do think that most of life's situations are covered in his works. I always observe what others are doing and wonder why they do what they do. I'm not a peeping Tom or anything like that. I'm just interested in and fascinated by the human condition. I really think that's why I love Shakespeare so much. I consider the Bard the greatest resource on the subject of the human condition. I have a personal relationship with him and with God. I know God is all about forgiveness and sometimes I think God speaks through the Bard. What would the Bard have to say about this? Remember that great speech in The Merchant of Venice. "The quality of mercy is not strained, it droppeth as the gentle rain from heaven upon the place beneath, it is twice blessed, it blesses him who gives and him who receives, it is mightiest in the mightiest; it becomes the throned monarch better than his crown." Shakespeare covered the waterfront when it came to talking about different kinds of people and their qualities.

What a contrast that speech is with Lady Macbeth. When she chastised her husband and tried to give him courage, she said, "I have given suck and know how tender it is to love the babe that milks me, I would while it was smiling in my face, have pluck'd my nipple from his boneless gums, and dashed the brains out, had I so sworn as you have done to this." Now, there's someone you wouldn't want to cross. I know these quotes because I used to teach high school English and sometimes they come in handy.

What I do hate is violence, more than anything else. I am the kind of guy who loves a happy ending. My wife once asked me if I would like to watch the movie Titanic with her. What for? I know how it ends and it's not good. Do I want to sit in a theatre and watch thousands of people go to their deaths? Is this going to make me feel enlightened when I leave the theatre? What's wrong with people? Why do they like tragedy so much?

Anyway, God will sort this out. I really want to forgive the old bastard. But I hate to tell you I'm not sorry he's dead, not because I wanted to see him punished but because he won't be able to hurt another kid the way he hurt me and who knows how many others.

But you know, what do you do when you are a twelve year old kid and you have this kind of secret festering away at you inside? How can you carry that load around with you? What can you do? I couldn't talk with my mom. Now, years later, I know that's what I should have done, although she did have a temper. But kids can't handle this kind of burden by themselves. I certainly wasn't going to tell my friends. The fact of the matter is that I felt guilty. For some reason or other I felt that it was my fault. And yes, there were times when I thought about suicide, times when I couldn't stand all the bad thoughts going through my head with no one to talk to. I used to pray to God to keep me alive until I was twenty one years old. I used to think that was the magic age of manhood and when I became a man I could deal with my problems. I didn't know it was going to affect me for the rest of my life. I mean, if I knew then what I know now, I don't know how I would have reacted. Kids are naturally optimistic. Don't you think, Doc? It's time that wears you down, chips away at the positive thinking until the old character reservoir fills up with negativity and cynicism. But you know what? I know fifty year old teenagers for God's sake. Some of them never grow up. Come to think of it, I'm a little like that, except I don't show it. I've worked very hard over the years to make myself look and act normal. But some older people, they don't even bother to try hiding their adolescence.

Chapter Five

Okay, so you want to know about my childhood. I already told you that my father died when I was five years old so I don't remember him. Although, sometimes I try like hell to recall any incident and in fact there were two that to this day I can recall. One was I was playing with a toy gun and I pretended to shoot him as he was sitting in his favourite chair. He pretended that I shot him and he slumped over in his chair. That's all I remember. Some memory, eh? All I know is I still have his favourite chair and there's no way that I could ever part with it. Sometimes, even now, I sit in the chair and I pretend that he is holding me. Anyway, I know he was a fun loving person who used to love telling jokes. I also know that, as a war veteran, he loved to hang out with his buddies at the Legion. He loved his beer and he loved to play cards, especially cribbage. Do you ever play cribbage, Doc?

The other incident I remember and I refer to this one in the poem I wrote about him was the touch of his hands. Funny thing to remember but I do recall having him wash my hands in the kitchen sink. His hands were so soft and gentle. Funny the things you remember. Oh yes, and there was one more thing. It happened in church when we there one Sunday for mass. During the confiteor when we would express our sorrow for our sins, every time we came to the mea culpa, he would touch his heart. I still miss him and hopefully, one day, if the good Lord is willing, I will get a chance to see him and talk with him.

As I said, he was a veteran of world war one, initially stationed in England but later transferred to Canada. I believe he met my mother in Halifax during the Halifax explosion. That was 1917. My mom who had moved to

Halifax from Fredericton, New Brunswick was working in a cannery two miles from the explosion when the windows of her factory were blown out. Imagine the enormity of that explosion. They say it was the biggest explosion ever next to Hiroshima. Anyway, thousands were killed and thousands more were injured during that terrible time.

Anyway, as I told you before, I don't like to dwell on tragedies. I am more interested in talking about my childhood. But you do need to know a bit of the background. We moved to Ontario after my father died. I don't know how my mom did it. She had three daughters and a boy. Yes, I was the baby of the family. Most of my life, all my relatives and friends of the family would refer to me as the baby of the family. I didn't really like that to tell you the truth. I mean who wants to be known as the baby of the family? Even when I became an adult, people used to call me that. Actually, there was another brother who died at the age of three from pneumonia. He would have been a lot older than me like my sisters. Anyway, he died before penicillin was invented. He's another one I want to meet when I get to heaven. Anyway, I can only imagine how upset my mom was. In fact, when I think about her losing her baby, I can almost hear her sobbing. Imagine losing a son like that. But that should give you an idea of how strong my mom was. She raised four children on her own. In fact, she took us away from what was familiar to her and tried to get a new start in a new province. I loved her for that.

As a kid, I guess I was always nodding off. It seemed I could never get enough sleep. My mom used to laugh when I did that. That was another thing about my mom. She used to laugh a lot, especially when someone else was the victim of some innocent act. I think she did this

51

because she was brought up during the vaudeville days when slapstick comedy was so popular. I must admit, though, I do nod off quite a bit even to this day. I guess I'm one of those guys who can power nap. I'm not a narcoleptic or anything like that. I knew a guy like that once. He could nod off anywhere, right in the middle of a conversation even. I was sitting with him in a pub watching the Toronto Maple Leafs play the Chicago Black Hawks in a playoff game. It was an exciting game but when I took my eye off the television, there was my friend with his head on the table, sleeping soundly. I'm not that bad.

Anyway, in my mom's eyes, I could do no wrong and every time my life swerved away from the beaten track or the normal way of living, she said that it was just another stage and that I had to grow up and face my problems and deal with them like a man.

Now I'm not saying my mom never worried about me. God knows I tested this theory countless times in my years with her. When I was five years old, after my dad died, I took off on a great adventure on my tricycle. We lived in a big city on a very busy road. I rode my bike a meandering eight miles, across busy thoroughfares, through unfamiliar neighbourhoods and across a long bridge over a ravine to my aunt's house. When I knocked on her door, she just about crapped, and phoned my mother immediately to calm her shattered nerves. Our neighbour, the local butcher and grocer, then shortly arrived to take me back home in his truck. Funny thing is I don't remember my mom ever getting upset about that one. I guess she was just happy to see that I was safe.

Well, anyway, I grew up at a time when it wasn't necessary to lock your doors. No one ever thought that their residence would be invaded or their lives would be violated in any way. So when my dad died, my sister, who was never known to have diplomacy, came up to my bedroom and told me, "you have to get up, dad just died." And that's how I heard about his death. I probably told you that before but it's one of those things that sticks out in my mind.

For the next few days, dad was laid out in our living room and every night before I went to bed, I had to kneel in front of him and say a prayer and then kiss his dead body. It was like kissing stone. I didn't like it. But now I know that the soul is really the principal of the body or another way of putting it I guess is that the body is a house for the soul but it is the soul that gives the body life. Once the soul leaves, the body dies. That's my belief anyway.

"When I ask you about your childhood, that's the first thing you remember, your dad dying? Do you have any really happy memories of being a kid?"

I could tell Granny didn't want me to dwell too long on the negative aspects of childhood but I wasn't exactly sure why. Maybe it had something to do with balance. You know, tragedies happen to all kids in one form or another, I think. But mostly being a kid should be about happy events.

Sure, I do. I remember how much fun I had as a kid. I used to love to play hockey. In fact, I played any sport there was. I just loved running and playing anything. I remember lacing up my skates in the house and skating along the sidewalk or road, wherever we could find a slippery surface, and then skating all the way to school. We had an outdoor hockey cushion in the schoolyard and we practically lived on it during the winter months. Fr.

Whiskers used to join us there. He was a great athlete. He could skate, punt a football a mile and hit a baseball even farther. He was a lot of fun to be around, if you want to know the real truth. Maybe it was because I lost my male role model, maybe that's the reason I enjoyed his company so much.

Anyway, often I would sit at my seat in the portable with my skates still on and when the bell rang for recess or for lunch I would take off and be the first one on the rink. I just loved the cold. I loved the hard ice surface. I loved the slap of the puck against the boards. I loved every thing about the game of hockey. I wasn't bad at it either, not a star but I delighted in playing the game. It was pure joy for me.

One time I played for an actual team. I forget the name of it now. I think it was Bruce's Automotive or something like that but anyway I remember we were supposed to go to Stouffville to play a game in their arena. It actually had a roof over it and I played there, inside, for the first time. I was probably ten or eleven. I also remember telling the coach that I couldn't go that day because I didn't have the quarter I needed to get in. He paid for me. I don't remember his name but I have never forgotten his kindness. He was a good role model for me. How often would I come home with my hands and feet frozen? How often did I thaw out against the register and then have a hot chocolate and then head out again for more fun? There's no doubt about it. In the winter months I was never cheated out of being a kid. This was a good time for me. I have plenty of happy memories of being a kid.

In the summer, we played in the park, practically lived there. We climbed trees, played hide and seek, swam wherever there was water. I remember there was a family in the north part of the city. It was rumoured that they had a backyard pool. So off we would go on our bikes and waiting for an opportunity, we would sneak into this huge backyard with a concrete pool and swim in it. We were never caught but boy did we have fun there. The truth probably is that the family that lived there was likely off in some exotic locale for a vacation, some place like Florida.

That was another thing when we were kids. I didn't know anyone who went South for the winter. I didn't even know anyone who owned a pool. Now it seems you can swim from one end of the city to the other just by hopping fences. There was no television then. So we didn't have commercials with little kids coming in from the cold saying, "I need a holiday and I need it bad." Then on the screen we see the same family frolicking on a beach in Florida. Kids don't need a holiday from the snow. Kids love the snow. Don't let television tell you what you should think. Anyway, the backyard pool wasn't far from Hog's Hollow, another favourite swimming hole. I remember swimming there for hours on one hot summer day and then walking another six miles home in the hot sun. That was the day I got sun stroke. Boy, was I sick! I loved swimming. Still do.

I don't want to get carried away with all of these happy stories but you did ask me. My favourite swimming story, though, happened during the exhibition. You know what the transit system was like during that time. I can tell you that everyone was in a festive mood, singing and loud talking on the buses and streetcars. Anyway, I was twelve years old and I was on my way to the exhibition. I was with my friend Jack Ripley, believe it or not. I just had to say that in case you didn't know who Ripley the magician was. That was the line he was always introduced by -

Ripley, believe it or not. Anyway, Jack was not a magician. He was just a friend, although he once showed me a card trick that was pretty neat. Jack and I were in the same grade together. In fact, we had been in the same grade since grade one.

We didn't have kindergarten in our school on account of it was a Catholic school. Only the Protestants had kindergarten in those days. But then again, they didn't get all the holidays that we got either. Holy days of obligation. What that meant was that every time there was a holy day we didn't have to go to school but we did have to go to mass. All Soul's day on November first and the Feast of the Immaculate Conception on December eight were two of them. Then there was the Feast of the Assumption but that took place in the summer but we still had to go to mass. When you think about it, holiday and holy day are almost the same word. They certainly had the same meaning for Catholic school kids when I was growing up.

Anyway, Jack lived down the street from me and we were like brothers. He could walk into my house and I into his and open the refrigerator door and help himself to milk or cookies and I could do the same at his house. His parents were like mine and my parents were like his and often we would stay over at one another's houses. We were both Catholics and went to the same church and served as altar boys together. Jack was very religious, probably the most moral person I knew. He always had an unshakeable opinion on right and wrong. In fact, when he finished high school, he entered the priesthood and studied for five years before finally leaving.

Did I already tell you about him? I guess I'm showing my age. Old people do that a lot, don't they? I mean they repeat themselves. Well, I don't really think of myself as being old. I have old friends who say that age is just a number. I'm sure to a young person, I'm old. Anyway, I don't know why Jack left the priesthood but he became a teacher, just like me. He eventually ended up in a northern town as principal of a high school. I found this out because I wrote him. I'll tell you more about that later. Anyway, where was I? Oh, yes, the exhibition and swimming.

Well, there we were, two twelve year old kids on our way down to the exhibition on the Bathurst Streetcar. In those days, parents thought nothing of letting their kids go off to the Ex on their own or anywhere on their own for that matter. This was a time when doors were left unlocked at night. Anyway, let me tell the story. If only I could learn to stop interrupting myself. The streetcar was really crowded and Jack found a seat at the back and I found a seat beside an older lady. That was another thing when we were kids. If ever we were sitting in a bus or a streetcar and an older person got on, we would get up and offer them our seat. That was automatic. Anyway, I don't know how old this older lady was. When you're twelve, I guess anyone more than thirty is quite old. But she was older than that. She was older than my mom. She might even have been fifty for all I know.

"Going to the Exhibition?"

"Yes ma'am."

"Going on all the rides, I suppose?"

"Yes ma'am, as many as we can."

"What's your favourite thing to do at the Ex?"

"I like the House of Horrors."

"You mean the one with the laughing lady in front of it?"

"Yes, that's the one."

"What is it you like about that one?"

"I don't know. I guess I just like being scared or something. You know when you're in there and it's all dark and something jumps out at you. It's kind of neat."

"Are you going in the swimming races today?"

"No ma'am. I didn't know about swimming races."

"Well, every year at the Ex, they have swimming races for all the young people in the city. And you never heard about them?"

"No ma'am, I never have."

"Do you like swimming?"

"Oh yes, ma'am, I love swimming."

"Well, why don't you go in the races today?"

"Well, for one thing I don't have a bathing suit with me."

"That won't be a problem. We'll get you one down there. I'll tell you what. If you go in a swimming race and win, I will give you a dollar."

Now I should explain that a dollar was a lot of money back in those days, Doc, as many will remember. It probably cost us no more than fifteen cents to get into the grounds in the first place, although Jack and I never paid because we knew where we could sneak in for nothing. A dollar? That could have paid for most of my day at the Ex. She definitely had my interest. Besides, I was a good swimmer and I had no doubt that I could give any kid my age a run for his money.

"A dollar if I win a race?" I asked.

"Yes, that's right. I just love to see young people being active in sports."

"Well, if you think I can."

Jack couldn't hear what was going on but you could tell he wanted to know because when I looked back at him, he kind of shrugged his shoulders and had a puzzled look on his face as if to ask "what's going on?"

Then the lady said, "I'm sure it will be fine. Oh, here's our stop. You just follow me now."

"Well," I said, " my friend Jack is coming too. He's back there and we usually go in another way."

Summing up the situation quickly, she just said, "follow me," so we did. And guess what? She paid to get both of us into the Ex and we made our way through the grounds and over to where the swimming events were to take place. Along the way, I was able to tell Jack what we were going to do and he said I was nuts. The lady even asked Jack if he wanted to go in the races with me and she even offered him the same deal but he declined. Jack tried to talk me out of it but it was no use. I was going to swim in a real race in Lake Ontario for the first time in my life.

Well, then we made our way over to the registration table where there was a lineup of kids. The lady told me I had to get in line and register and I would be told what I had to do next. She said that she would be sitting somewhere near the finish line and would be looking for me after the race. Jack was with me and we strained to hear what the man behind the registration desk was saying to the kids in front of me. Then it became clear, as he asked each one the same question.

"What swim club do you swim for and who is your coach?"

Swim club? Coach? The only place I ever swam was in Hogs Hollow or the Y and I never had a coach. Anyway, I was next in line. Then the desk man, without even looking up, his pen poised on an official sheet of paper, said,

"What is your name?"

"Mike Carroll," I lied. I had all kinds of aliases.

"What club do you swim with?"

I hesitated. He noticed. And then he looked at me for the first time.

"The North Toronto Y, sir."

"North Toronto Y, eh? Who's your coach?"

"Mr. Whiskers, sir."

"Mr. Whiskers is the name of your swim coach?"

"Yes sir."

This wasn't going too well. The desk man was doubting me, I could tell.

"Well, I'm looking at my list here and I don't see anyone else from the North Toronto Y. And I don't know of any coach by the name of Whiskers."

I kept thinking about the dollar I was promised.

"Sir, I really want to be in this race and I know I can do it."

"Well son, you're not really in a swimming club are you?"

"No sir," I said with my head now down.

"Tell me why you want to go in this race today then."

I told him the story, how I met the lady on the Bathurst streetcar and how she promised me a dollar if I won the race and how much she liked to see kids playing sports. And guess what? The desk man said it was okay, that he was going to allow me to enter the race.

"Next."

I didn't move.

"On your way now son before it's too late and I change my mind."

"Well sir, there's one more thing."

"What's that?"

"I don't have a bathing suit with me because I wasn't going to go in the race."

He looked at me like I was crazy and in a way I suppose I was but I told him we were just going to have some fun at the Ex on the rides and stuff and I didn't think I would get a chance to go in a real swim race.

Then he hollered so everyone around could hear.

"Anybody here got an extra bathing suit they can lend this kid?"

He said that pretty loudly too. Jack and I were kind of embarrassed. At least I was. Jack was more certain than ever now that I was crazy. I kept thinking about the dollar. Some of the other kids started to laugh. I didn't care. As old Macbeth once said, "I'm steeped in blood too far that to return would be as tedious as to go o'er," or something like that. I tell you that Shakespeare covered just about everything.

Anyway, a girl came up and handed me her bathing suit. It wasn't a bikini either. It was a girl's one piece bathing suit. The kids laughed even louder. The girl didn't laugh. You could tell she was serious. You could tell she was kind of nice, actually. I took the suit and was shown where the change room was. I slipped into the suit and kept thinking about the dollar because if it wasn't for that, I never would have done what I did. As soon as I stepped outside, the whistles started and the laughter grew in volume. I didn't care. I kept thinking about the dollar. I made my way down to the lake and found the pier. My race was announced.

"And at the far end, Mike Carroll from the North Toronto Y."

It sounded like I received the biggest ovation.

I was at the end of the pier. I wanted to be as far away from people as I could and I couldn't wait for the race to start so I could get into the water, away from the stares of the curious onlookers. I saw Jack at the far end of the other pier where the race was finished and I even saw the lady in the crowd at the far end as well.

"On your mark, get set," and at the sound of a starting gun, "go."

Have you ever immersed your body into the waters of Lake Ontario, Doc? This was my first time and it was cold, colder than I had ever anticipated. It was like diving into a pool of melting ice cubes. I had an adrenalin rush like you wouldn't believe and I tore across that water as fast as I could. Half way to the finish line, I sneaked a peak to my right and noticed that I was well in the lead, well ahead of the other twelve contestants. But then something dreadful happened. My arms started to feel like lead and my breathing became more rapid and shallow. I started to take in water as, one by one, the other swimmers passed me. I finally made it to the other side, finishing last in the race.

All I could think of was that damn dollar. But I was exhausted and had to be pulled out of the water. I lay on my back a moment until the lady stood over me and asked if I was okay. I told her I was sorry that I didn't win the race but she said it was okay and gave me the dollar anyway. The desk man congratulated me on my efforts and suggested that, for the next time, I should probably train for the event and get myself a good coach and maybe even join a real swim club. He winked as he walked away, disappearing into the crowd. After giving the bathing suit back to the kind girl, Jack and I headed off to the midway for an afternoon of fun. I don't think I will ever forget the kindness of those three people who came into my life unexpectedly and disappeared from it just as abruptly. An old lady, an older man who was registering kids for the swim and a young girl. People can be really nice at times.

I tell you these stories because I want you to know that I really enjoyed being a kid. Besides, you asked me to tell you about happy stories of my childhood. To tell you the truth, I had so much fun being a kid but my emotional and psychological growth came to a grinding halt that Fall in the basement of the church where we played floor hockey. Did you ever play that game? Girls used to play it too. You used a stick that went inside the round felt puck that had a hole in the middle. It was great fun. There were nets at either end of the room.

Chapter Six

Granny looked up over her glasses at me and said, "Okay, today's the day."

"I know and I'm not too happy about it."

"How do you feel?"

"I'm embarrassed, if you really want to know."

"You know that's normal enough. But you also know that you need to tell me. You need to get it out in the open so you can start dealing with it, start dealing with your feelings. Are you okay with that?" The archaeologist was about to hit pay dirt.

"It's hard, you know."

I couldn't believe my voice was breaking. Granny said nothing. She just nodded.

"When I think of how it happened, it all seems so real. My God, Doc, it was forty five years ago!"

Another nod from Granny.

"I can still smell his after shave lotion. Is that normal?"

She smiled and said, "yes, it is. Often when something so traumatic happens, you are able to visualize easily and your senses become much more alert. So yes what you are saying is very normal."

We used to play floor hockey every Friday night in the church hall. Fr. Whiskers used to supervise. There were a lot of kids there and everyone looked forward to it. One night, after our game, Fr. Whiskers asked me if I would stay behind for a few minutes. I told him that I came with Jack and I should probably go home with him. He then told Jack to go on ahead and that he, Fr. Whiskers that is, would drive me home a little later. God's representative here on earth, right? I heard that all my life. We had implicit faith in and respect for the priests. So whatever he said, that's what we did. Anyway, Jack left and there was no one in the church hall except Fr. Whiskers and me. He invited me into a small room to have a talk. He closed the door and asked how I was doing, how my family was doing, all the while stroking my hair. Yes, I was uncomfortable but he was God's representative, right? Then sitting on the front of the small desk, he put his arm around me and twirling me around so my back was facing him, he pulled me close to his body. He kept talking about nothing, murmuring was more like it, as he rubbed my cheek with his whiskers. God's fucking representative, right? I can still smell his cologne and can still feel his whiskers. I tried to break loose but he had me in a vice grip and I couldn't move. I told him to please stop but he kept going. He said that he really liked me, in fact that he loved me and he wanted me to feel his love. All I could feel was his prick against my ass and his hand down the front of my pants. God's goddamn fucking representative, right? He put his hand on my dick and started to rub it and then he pulled down my pants and I could feel his dick against my ass. He held me like that and I couldn't move. His hand was like an iron bar against my stomach. Then he started pushing into me and I was crying and I asked him to stop and he wouldn't stop. He just kept pushing into me and then I felt wet at the back and finally, he let go of my dick and released me from his grasp. He told me I wasn't to say anything to anybody. I was sobbing. He told me everything would be fine now. I slowly stopped crying. He told me again not to say anything to anyone, that he was my priest and my special friend and if I told anyone no one would believe me anyway. He told me he would always be there to help me. He told me again that he loved me. Finally, I collected myself and told him I had to go. He said he would drive me and I said no thanks, I would rather walk home. He said are you sure and I said yes I was sure. I told him I was okay now, that I had to go. On my way home, I cried. I didn't know what to do, Doc. I couldn't possibly tell my mother. It would kill her. Besides, Fr. Whiskers was God's representative on earth, right? So, I resolved to say nothing. I wouldn't tell anyone, not even my friend Jack. No one would ever know. What had I done to make this happen? This was my fault.

The next day was Saturday and I had to go to confession. We went to confession every Saturday whether we had to or not. How was I going to explain this to the priest? Naturally, I wouldn't go to Fr. Whiskers any more for confession. I would have to go to Fr. Murray who was partially deaf anyway. I wouldn't tell him either. I would just make up my usual confession of six lies and five taking the Lord's name in vain and whatever else came up that was normal in the life of a twelve year old boy. But no one would ever know about this incident. No one would know - ever! The next day, Jack came to call and right away noticed I wasn't quite myself. My mom said I looked a little pale and took my temperature. It was okay. She told me to take it easy on that day, that even for a twelve year old I was far too active and that I should just slow down for that day.

The next Friday it happened again. Only this time I was ready, I thought. When Fr. Whiskers held me in his vice grip, I asked him what if I was destined to be a saint or a special angel. How would that make him feel? I said this because I thought maybe he wouldn't do what he did again. I thought it would make him pause, give him something to think about, being a priest and all. He asked me why I thought I could be a special angel anyway. I said well God loves us all, right? You see what I was trying to do? A twelve year old kid trying to reason with a priest, trying to lay a guilt trip on him, instead of the other way around, trying to get him to stop. But it didn't work and he did it again, just like the last time. You ask why did I continue to go back to that place every week? I was twelve years old. What did I know about life? It was my life at that time. That's what we did every week and to suddenly stop would just bring attention and I didn't want that. More than anything else, I didn't want that. Then one night, I heard someone struggling in that little room. He had someone else in there. That son of a bitch. I took off. But the next week I heard the noise again.

Life went on for me. I kept the secret deep inside of me and tried to be as normal as possible. I spoke to God a lot, asked Her to watch over me, asked Her to protect me, asked Her to love me and to stay with me always. I had nothing else to do. I could only talk to God. Twelve years old and all of a sudden, it seemed, I was thirty years old. But I never knew how to control my emotions. My emotional level and development stopped when I was twelve years old. I was an emotional cripple, that's what I was. Mostly, I am not that way anymore, thanks to you Granny, but mostly thanks to my wife.

Now I know you want to know if I ever told her. Does she know what happened to me so many years ago? This bullshit happened to me when I was twelve. I told my wife when I was fifty eight. She was the first one to ever know my secret. Well, not exactly the first but I will get to that later. But you know what? My wife was actually relieved when I told her. You know why? I'll tell you. Anytime she ever approached me for intimacy, I would recoil and tell her I didn't feel like it. She thought I did that because she was not attractive to me. The truth is that I had to be the one in control, the only one who could initiate intimacy. Can you imagine what I put her through all those years? Talk about having an effect on your relationships. Why did I wait so long to tell her you ask? Because, it was buried so deep inside of me and I kept so busy throughout my whole career that I never thought about it. And that's the truth. When I retired, I started to reflect on my life and its past and it seemed day by day, this horrible trauma began to get closer to the surface. Now that I have told you, I feel like a diver who has descended to the bottom of the ocean and has just shot up to the surface gasping for air.

Chapter Seven

As the months passed, this trauma began to recede deeper and deeper into my subconscious. Do you think the brain just has this ability to push away bad experiences, Doc? I know I had to go to an opthamologist recently because I was seeing what he called floaters and was experiencing flashes of light in the dark. He told me what it was and that the brain would eventually learn to ignore it.

Anyway, at first, I became quite sullen and withdrawn. This gloomy mood change would come back to haunt me too many times in future years. My mother saw the change happening in me and attributed it to puberty, becoming a teenager. It was just a stage that I was going through. All teenagers do that, especially boys. That's all it was, a stage. My personality started to change as well. I was always very gregarious and considered to be precocious in my development. But my relationships with others changed also. Jack, who was like a brother to me, didn't like the way I was changing. He knew something had happened. I didn't see him as much anymore. But one day we talked about it.

He just came right out and said, "how come you changed so much?"

I said, "my mom says it's a stage I'm going through."

"You mean like when you become a teenager."

"Yeah."

"That's bullshit. And you know it. That hasn't happened to me."

"Well it doesn't happen to everyone at the same time."

"No way, man, you've changed and it's not because of changing into a teenager."

"Well, what do you think it is then, smart ass?"

"I remember when you started to change. It was right when we were playing floor hockey. How come? What happened?"

"Mind your own business Jack."

"See what I mean. You never used to tell me that."

"Yeah, so what? Anyway, I told you before, it's a stage. My mom says I'm just going through a stage, that's all. When you're going through a stage, you gotta start somewhere."

"Well anyway, I don't believe it's a stage. Man, if that's what happens when you become a teenager, I never want to become a teenager."

"Well, it's too late now. You're already thirteen."

"Yeah I know but it freaks me out man."

"Forget about it, Jack. Let's just not talk about it anymore, okay?"

"Yeah...okay. What do you want to talk about anyway?"

"We don't have to talk about anything. Just shut up, okay."

"Man, this is freaky. Anyway, this is our last year in grade school. Where're we going to go next year to high school?"

"Across the street maybe?"

"You mean Northern?"

"Yeah, why not?"

"You always said you wanted to go to St. James, the boys' school. Now all of a sudden you don't want to go there?"

"Nope."

"Why not?"

"I told you what happened to my cousin there. Anyway, I don't want to, that's all. Look, can we just talk about something else for a change?"

"Like what?"

"Shirley Wood's having a party at her place for all the grade eights. You going to go?"

"I guess so."

"She's pretty neat you know."

"What do you mean?"

"She has a nice body."

"I don't get you. First you say you're going through a stage. You don't talk to your mom hardly anymore. You get mad at me and now you're talking about a girl's body."

"I told you, it's a stage. Besides, I like thinking about girls' bodies. What's wrong with that?"

"Another thing, your marks aren't as good as they used to be."

"Look Jack, can we stop talking about all this? It's really starting to bug me. I'll see you later."

Jack was pretty smart. I guess you would say he was intuitive. He knew something had happened to me but he never said anything more about it. Whenever his mother asked why I never came around anymore, he just said I was going through a stage. At least that's what my mother used to say. I didn't see much of him after that. He went to the boys' school and, to tell you the truth, I didn't feel like hanging out with him any more. Being a teenager was a difficult time for me. In fact, the older I got the more difficult it became. In fact, I would have to say, in looking back on it, my teenage years were easily the most difficult of my entire life.

Granny said, "whatever happened to your friend Jack?"

"Remember I told you that he studied to be a priest and that he eventually went into teaching, like me. Well, the last I heard was that he had become a principal of a high school in a small town up north."

"Did you ever see him again?"

"I haven't seen him for years. Why are you asking me about Jack anyway?"

Then it dawned on me again.

"You think he was abused too, don't you?"

"There's a good chance of that, yes. Anyway, I just wondered if you had ever talked with him after all of these years."

"No, I'm not very good at keeping my friends. I lost touch with him but I always wanted to talk with him again. We were very close as kids."

"Why don't you write him?"

"Maybe I will."

I knew what she was getting at. She wanted me to find out if he was abused too.

"Can we stop for now, Doc? I have a headache."

"That's fine but I want you to do something for next week."

"What's that?"

"I want you to write a letter to Fr. Whiskers."

"Well, Doc, he's dead now."

"Doesn't matter. Write it as though he is still alive. I'll go over it with you next week."

"What do you want me to say?"

"Whatever you feel like saying."

I thought about what Granny had said on my drive home and I couldn't get Jack out of my mind. I decided to try to get in touch with him. I don't know why after all these years. Sure, it would be good to see him again but mostly I wanted to know more about his childhood. I really wanted to know if he too had been abused by Fr. Whiskers. I think knowing someone else who had the same experience would help me. At least, it might validate my childhood and the way that I had felt all these years. Granny, boy, she was sly. I bet she knew I would have this conversation with myself.

I remember leaving her office that day feeling exhausted. I came face to face with my past in all of its ugliness and repulsiveness and I felt whipped. I don't even remember the drive home. All I could think of was my friend Jack. I don't know why but I couldn't get him out of my mind. I know that Granny asked me to write to Fr. Whiskers but instead I decided to write to Jack. I would get around to Fr. Whiskers later.

Chapter Eight

Dear Jack

I hardly know where to start. It seems so long ago and yet it seems like yesterday when we hung out together as kids. I married a beautiful girl from the Maritimes and we raised three beautiful children. They're all married now and have given us five grandchildren. They keep us young and have more than made up for the school kids I taught over the years who used to have a similar effect on me. I know you're retired now as am I. And I don't know about you but I have had so much time to think about my life and so much of my childhood seems to have resurfaced. I was remembering how we used to play ball together and hockey in the winter. They were good times for the most part.

Do you remember how much time we spent at the church? Do you remember how much we loved to play floor hockey in the church basement? Fr. Whiskers. Did you ever see him again? I know you must have heard that he was murdered. It's been all over the news. That man had a profound effect on my life and I wondered if he affected you in the same way. I often think about you and about those days. And I wonder what your life has been like. I knew that you had studied for years to be a priest and when you left, you went into teaching. I think we had similar paths. In fact, I think we have very much in common, probably more than we realize. Would you ever consider meeting up one day? I would love to see you. Now that you're retired, like me, do you think about your past life? Do you ever think about those days? Give me a call or write, your old childhood friend, B.

I told Granny what had I had done in the week since my last visit. As always, she listened attentively. I know she was convinced that Jack had been violated like me. But I had to find out for myself. I can't explain why I felt this way. I just did.

Anyway, Doc, I was afraid that if I waited too long I wouldn't send the letter so I mailed it right away. Three days later, Jack phoned me. I couldn't believe it. His voice was the same and he seemed happy to talk with me. He said he had lost track of me and was so elated to receive my letter and that he would love to see me. It was a three hour drive to his house and I decided if it was okay with him that I would go to visit him the following day. I told my wife about it and seeing my excitement, she agreed that reacquainting with an old friend was sure to help me in unravelling my past. It was Friday morning and I knew I would be seeing you on Monday. We would have much to talk about.

All the way up in the car, I thought about how Jack and I used to be like brothers. We played in the same park as kids, played on the same ball team. He was a pitcher and I caught. He was a lefty and could throw some heaters. He also had a curve ball that he mixed in just to keep the opposing batters off guard. We went to the same school and the same church. His house was mine and mine was his. We were inseparable. I wondered what kind of a life he'd had. Was it anything like mine? Was he happy? It would be great to meet his wife and family. I could hardly wait. With those thoughts and the sounds of Peter Appleyard on the vibes accompanying me, I made my way up north.

Soon the scenery changed, more pine trees, more lakes and not nearly as much traffic. I passed by the deer farm that you could see right off the highway. It was weird seeing deer like that. How could the farmer keep them all in that one area? Glancing over, I noticed a collie, making its way out to the field with its master. I would like to have stopped to see what it was going to do but I was anxious to meet up with my long lost friend. I settled for thinking about my own collies, especially Prince.

I was remembering the times in the summer, on those hot sultry days when he used to lie on our front step and keep an eye on the neighbourhood. He would be enjoying his reverie when a strange dog or a strange person, for that matter, would enter into his territory. One eye would open and he would emit a low gutteral sound. He was just protecting his own turf and his own family. That's the way dogs are. If I had my way, I would allow dogs to be canonized. That's how strongly I feel about them. I mean they will easily give up their lives for their masters, without hesitation. All they want to do is love and be loved in return, just the way God wants the rest of us to be.

Anyway, I soon arrived in Jack's town and before long found his street. There he was, sitting on his verandah. He was waiting for me. I could see him watching me as I pulled into his driveway. Honest to God, he looked like an aged beach bum, still muscular looking, with a lined face and shockingly white curly hair. He was a handsome man and I would have known him anywhere. He stood when he saw me get out of the car and came down the steps to greet me. He put his arms out to hug me but was taken slightly aback when I offered him my hand, preferring to shake hands. We greeted heartily and sat down together on his front porch. His wife was pulling out of his driveway, apparently on her way to visit an old relative. At first, it seemed like a coincidence that I pulled in just as she was pulling out but I knew the real reason why she was leaving. Jack stopped her and introduced her to me.

I went over and shook her hand through the open window of her car. I knew she was leaving so that the two of us would have time together.

After exchanging information on our past lives and our wives and our children and our children's children, Jack brought up my letter. He had read between the lines and wanted me to fill in the blanks. I told him about my experience with Fr. Whiskers and he cried. I couldn't believe how easily he started to weep. I took his hand and told him it was okay, that I was dealing with it. But then he sort of shocked me when he said that he had kept in touch with Fr. Whiskers over the years and that they had maintained a friendship. He said that he had no idea of his perversion.

He wanted to know more and I told him about you, Doc, that I was seeing you on a regular basis, and do you know what he said to me? He told me that he was going to a shrink also and that he had clinical depression. He also told me that he drank too much. I know you think he was abused too but he denied it.

Anyway, we spent the day together, sharing many of our experiences. We had so much to talk about. I asked him about his religion. He told me he no longer practised his religion. When I asked him why, he told me that if I ever brought it up again he would never speak to me again. Maybe I already told you that. Anyway, his response shocked me but also made me realize that there was much more to this man than he was telling me. Like you, I became convinced that he had experienced the same fate as I many years ago in that church basement. He always denied it but his wife at one point, later in the day, hinted that she knew the truth. He further told me that if he were me, he would have visited Fr. Whiskers and kicked

79

the shit out of him. Honest to God, those were his words. He said it with such anger.

All the way home, I thought about Jack. I knew he had a troubled past, perhaps greater than mine. But how could he so vehemently deny being molested and why did he react so strongly when I asked him about his religion? Also, what made him cry so easily when I told him about my experiences? After all these years, those encounters in the church basement were so fresh in my mind. I suspected that he could recall similar incidences just as vividly.

That night I had a dream. It was more like a nightmare. I woke up in a sweat. I told you I was in the habit of writing down the details of my dreams. I'm happy that I did so I could relate them to you, Doc. I dreamt that I was in a room and I couldn't get out. There was a window there and I could see the outside if I stood up on my toes. There was a light coming through the window. I stood on a chair and tried to bash the window but it wouldn't break. I felt someone grab at my legs. It was Fr. Whiskers. I kicked him and ran up against the door. It wouldn't budge. I punched him but he didn't even flinch. I yelled for him to stay away but he reached for me and put his arm around me and held me in that vice grip of his and I began to sob when I felt someone nudging me from behind and I awoke. It was my wife. She was scared for me and couldn't understand. I told her I had to write down the details and then I told them to her. We both tried to figure out what that dream had meant but we couldn't. Oh, we knew it was related to my visit with Jack but we both agreed that you were the one to interpret it. I told my wife about Jack and Fr. Whiskers when we were kids and how I thought maybe Jack had been abused too.

Now I need to speak directly to you, the reader. Granny told me that this dream was a reflection of my fear and of the way I felt about Fr. Whiskers and the abuse. Given the number of years that had elapsed between that time and now, the dream was proof that I had never been able to escape from its reality and from its effects. Trying to get out of that room was my trying to rid myself of the memory and reliving that trauma and facing up to it was the only way to do that. The window and the light beyond was a good sign. She seemed to think that this reflected hope and a way out of my dilemma. Probably she thought that by visiting with Jack and feeling his pain and anguish, I was on my way to unravelling my past and coming to grips with it. She cautioned that I could have similar dreams in the weeks and months to come depending on how I was feeling.

In all, Granny was pleased with my progress thus far. She especially appreciated the letter that I had written to Jack and said that writing my thoughts was a way of externalizing them, of extracting them from my subconscious mind. In that way, I could begin the healing process. I could begin to deal with my problem after all of these years.

"However, there is one thing I would like to ask you and make a comment on. It's hard enough being an adolescent boy, having to deal with normal sexual and emotional developments. How could you have possibly kept your secret through a time like that?"

Once again the Irish leprechaun illustrated her insightfulness.

Ken Hills

Chapter Nine

I need to tell you also, Doc, that my drinking really began at a young age. I have never considered myself an alcoholic but I always felt like the booze had a calming effect on me. I have already told you that I had my dark days and they stayed with me for my entire life. Also, however, I would often feel agitated and tense. Whenever I felt like that and I had an opportunity to drink, I would. It was easy enough to access alcohol even at my young age. My stepfather who left home when he was only thirteen years old had no problem offering me a beer. I forgot to tell you that my mom remarried when I was fifteen but more about that later. Anyway, I already told you that my mom had no problem with the drinking as long as I confined it to the home. Well, that made it easier for me but I have to admit that I didn't confine it to the home. Whenever there was a school dance, someone would always bring a mickey and would be willing to share. Eventually, I had my own mickey and never had trouble filling it. Like finds like, eh Doc? One time a school chum told me that he knew of a hotel downtown that would allow underage drinkers. I mean they didn't advertise this fact but, apparently, if you remained low key in the bar, maybe sat in an out of the way corner, you could be served a beer. I decided to check it out for myself.

Well, I found this out of the way hotel in the downtown area of the city, and my friend was right. I had no trouble being served. Besides, even though I was just a seventeen year old kid, I looked much older than I really was, especially since I had sprouted a moustache. I sort of liked the moustache to tell you the truth. Maybe it was like a disguise. Who knows? Like one of my students once who wore her hair in such a way that it hid half of her face and covered her eyes. I asked her about it and she told me that it was her disguise. She called it her "curtain on the world." She could look out at the world any time she wanted to. I knew what she meant about all that. Anyway, I liked my moustache and I also liked to drink, and I liked going to Jake's. That was what the pub was called, after the owner, another Newfy, just my luck. More about that later. It was like going into someone's house.

First of all, it was a distraction in my life and I needed that, sometimes worse than at others. So I drank and sat in the dark corner of this neighbourhood pub, away from the bustling and hustling of the world. Sort of like my student. I sat in a dark corner and looked out at the world, away from the crowds, away from my family and any friends that I had left. Because that happens too, you know, Doc. It's easy to lose friends when you've been abused and your life has been derailed and your human compass has been put off its normal course. So, I got to the point in my life where I stopped trying to make friends and became what some would call a loner. That was okay. I didn't mind being a loner. It made me feel safe, like no one was approaching me, no one was sizing me up as an easy prey. I had developed a shield and no one would ever see behind it. No one would ever violate me again.

Then one day, Mary came into my life. Mary was a prostitute, Doc, the first one I had ever met. It's hard for me to tell you that because I am afraid that you will prejudge me. God, I hate it when people do that. Are you thinking I must have been really bad to take up with a prostitute? I can sense a little discomfort but I must admit, Doc, I've never met anyone so stoical. I don't know what you're thinking but I think that it is not very nice.

Oh, maybe it's just me again. I often project my feelings on to others. Anyway, let me explain. Holden sought the company of a prostitute too, don't you remember? And we're practically brothers. He just wanted to talk with somebody, just like me. But with him, it was very impersonal and brief. I wanted a personal relationship with this prostitute because, well, it would be sort of like having a shrink, you know what I mean? It just seemed like a good idea, you know, to have somebody to talk with, who had to listen because I would be paying her. I wasn't looking for sex. Honest to God! I just wanted a captive audience, someone who had to listen and maybe someone who could give me a little bit of advice. That's all I was looking for, in case you're thinking anything different. I mean I still liked sex. I was a teenager after all. Just like other boys, I had my moments with teenage girls. But I swear to God this wasn't about sex.

I know you probably think this was the wrong thing to do but I couldn't talk with anyone else. Well, I guess I could have but I didn't want to. It was just too embarrassing and I sure wasn't going to let my family know I was seeing a prostitute. How do you think they would react to that? Personally, I thought it was a good idea but I don't think my mom would have liked it. I wonder how Mary, the mother of Jesus, would have reacted if Jesus brought Mary Magdalene home with him and introduced her to his mother? "Hi Mom, this is my friend Mary. She's a prostitute." You know what, though? She would have been okay with that. Granted, she knew who her son really was but he was a human being too. Come to think of it, my mom would have been okay with it too. She was special and she would have understood. Unfortunately, you really have to watch what you say these days. I mean I love kids, you know. But I wouldn't go around saying that. Would you?

I should say that the early years of high school were okay. I played football and basketball and I know now that it was a perfect outlet for me at the time. I still used to get those down days, you know, days when I didn't want to talk to anyone, when I didn't want to be bothered with anything. But I kept up with my prayers, talking with God whenever I was too low. I really think that's what pulled me through those years.

Anyway, what does a seventeen year old kid know about life? Mary taught me plenty. Yes, I was seventeen when I first met her. I was looking for someone, anyone who could help me and as I learned later in my life, like water, we all settle at a level equal to our own. We seek out others who are like us. Sometimes, without having any factual knowledge, we can sense their presence. If you don't believe me, just look in at a high school cafeteria some time. The blacks sit together, the brightest kids sit together, the Italians sit together. Hell, it's like that in any city too. There are ethnic communities all over the place. People just like the comfort of being with others like themselves. In the same way, the emotionally crippled seek one another as if knowing that somehow the common denominator that unites them will ensure empathy and understanding, maybe even offer them a way out of their maze of difficulties.

There's a lot of truth in that, you know, because even as a teacher, I had to give my best effort to understand the kids in front of me. It was important that I knew where they were coming from because only then could I effectively communicate. They had to know that I was human too, just like them, oh a little older for sure but on the same human conveyor belt. I was just a little farther down the line. I keep telling you we should be more like dogs and just accept one another no matter what. Anyway, I used to tell the kids that there are many obvious truths in life and one of them was that many of them were more intelligent than I and some day would be smarter than I. But for the present because I had lived longer, read more, experienced more of life, I was smarter. But I'm off topic again, aren't I? Where was I? Oh yes Mary.

But Mary was different and I'm not sure how to describe her. She never really dressed like the typical prostitute, you know, tons of makeup, high heels, tight fitting clothes. Mary still had a softness about her face, still a sparkle in her eyes, a round, angelic looking face with penetrating brown eyes.

You can tell a lot about people by looking into their eyes. If you look hard enough, you can see their soul. Some were sad looking and you could tell that life had beaten them down along the way. Mary's soul was still very much alive and sparkling. She was wearing makeup but not excessively and her clothes were clean. It was just one of those chance meetings. When we looked at one another, there was an immediate connection. That's the thing with me. If I meet a person, I look them square in the face and I can tell from the start if I'm going to like them or not. It's almost like shaking hands with someone.

Some people have a vice grip for a handshake while others will give you a wet fish. Still others will give you two fingers or some may just grab your fingers before you can take proper hold of them. That's what I call the preemptive handshake. The preemptive shake is my least favourite. I prefer the ones who place their hand comfortably in yours, don't try to control you or strong arm you, just shake comfortably. Anyway, Mary came over to my table and asked if she could sit down. I said yes.

She said, "you're pretty young to be in here, aren't you?"

"No one seems to mind. Do you?" I said trying to project an air of maturity.

"I guess it's really none of my business. It's just unusual, that's all."

I didn't like being put on the defensive, so I said, "what about you? You don't look that old yourself?"

"Listen, are you looking for some action?"

"You mean with you?

"Yeah, sure, why not?"

"What kind of action?"

"What do you want?"

"Can we just talk?"

"Look kid, I don't have time for talk."

"I've got money." I flashed some money at her. "How much do you want?"

"Time is money for me, kid. So, you just want to talk?"

"Yes, I'd really like that."

"It'll cost you."

"I don't care. It would be nice to have someone to talk to."

"Let's go."

I followed Mary to an upstairs room in the pub. Jake, the owner, had a dog too. Its name was Ralph. It was a Heinz 57 variety with some collie in it as evidenced by its long nose. Every once in a while Jake would say R-r-r-ralph and it would come out like a bark. Anyway, this was another cool dog because he used to lay at the top of the stairs and prevent anyone from going up there. Except he knew Mary and he would just wag his tail as she walked by. He gave me the once over too, sniffing me as dogs do. I guess he found me acceptable as he lay back down at the top of the stairs. Mary opened a door and invited me in. She started to take her clothes off and I could see that she wasn't wearing a bra. To tell you the truth, I was embarrassed.

"Do you mind not taking your clothes off please?"

"You're really serious about just wanting to talk."

"Yeah, I am. I just want someone to talk to, someone who can understand and who will listen to me."

"What's the matter, don't you have a family?"

"Yeah, I do but I can't talk to them about everything, you know. I can talk to them about school, about some of the other kids they know but the really important stuff that I keep inside I can't talk to them about that."

"But you don't even know me. I'm a prostitute for God's sake. Do you even know how I make a living?"

"Yeah, I do but somehow I think we are a little bit the same and I was hoping."

"Listen kid, I'm not a shrink. Why don't you just take your money and go to a real shrink?"

"I can't do that. My family would know for sure what was going on. I don't want anyone I know to know about stuff, you know?"

"Look kid, you're wasting my time."

"I told you I'd pay you. How much do you want? I've got thirty bucks. Here it's yours."

Mary took the money and settled in a chair opposite mine.

"Okay kid, I can give you a few minutes. Talk."

"What's your name?"

"Mary, what's yours?"

"I'd rather not say. Do you mind?"

"You afraid I'm going to tell someone about you? What's your problem?"

"No, it's not that. I just feel better that way."

"Is that why you have a moustache? Are you trying to hide from people?"

I could tell by that remark that Mary was a very intuitive person.

"Yeah, I guess, something like that. Do you mind?"

"Whatever."

"Why do you do this, Mary?"

"None of your damn business. I thought you wanted to talk about your problems."

"I do, I do but first I just wanted to know a little more about you."

"Well forget that. If you want to talk, go ahead."

"I can't just come right out and tell you what I want. I need to know more about you first."

"Look, kid, this is getting too weird. Don't you have any friends you can talk to? Do you really have to come to a prostitute to talk about your problems?"

"Mary, I don't have any friends I can talk to about this. That's why I'm paying you for God's sake. I don't want sex from you. I just want you to listen. I already paid you thirty bucks. Why can't you do as I say anyway? I know it's not what you usually do but can't you listen to me for a little while?"

She looked at me, sort of like she was seeing me for the first time. It was a while before she spoke as though she were summing up the situation. Then she said. "All right kid, I'll listen but not today, okay? Besides your time is up."

"What do you mean?

"Just what I said. If you want to see me again, just let me know and I'll be here."

I returned to the pub and took my seat in the corner, avoiding the all knowing gazes of a few of the regular bar customers. I thought about Mary. I was guessing that she was a listener. No, maybe hoping is a better word. Not everyone is, you know what I mean.

Of course, Doc, you know what I mean. Shrinks have to be listeners. That's what they get paid to do and that's what they're trained for.

But most people are not good listeners. I can always tell. If I start talking to someone and they're looking right at me and then all of a sudden their eyes glaze over, I swear to God you could probably say anything and they would nod approval. "Your fly's open. Why don't you zip up? Uh, huh. Or you're drooling all over your chin. God that makes you look so ugly. Uh huh." I think it is worse now than it's ever been and I blame it all on television. Television teaches you how to be non responsive, you know what I mean? Sometimes when someone is engrossed in a television program, you almost have to strip to get their attention. Not that I would ever do that but you know what I mean. Honest to God, it's really a problem. That's why when I find a good listener, like you Doc, I'm so happy. So to pay a prostitute to listen makes sense to me. I mean if she stops listening or she's not good at it, then you just don't pay her, that's all. But I could tell Mary was a listener. She made a very good impression on me. I could hardly wait to see her again.

Life went on as usual for the next week. Oh, there was a fight at school one day but it didn't last too long. One of the Italian students made fun of a French Canadian. He called him a stupid Frog and the Frenchman countered with dumb Dago or something like that. Anyway, they threw a few fists and one of them got a bloody nose. But some of their friends broke it up, congratulating each contender for being so macho. What a lot of bullshit that is! Like what happened in that fight was like a microcosm of what goes on everywhere, you know what I mean? People fighting over racial issues, people fighting over religious issues. It makes no sense to me at all.

Anyway, I spent some time in the local pool hall. I really liked the atmosphere to tell you the truth. I liked the smoke and the noise, the crack of the balls.

"Two banks in the corner," someone would say.

"How did you put so much English on that ball? "said another.

"Play you for five bucks."

It was fun, you know, and a good distraction for me. School was okay too I guess, although I must admit I did a fair bit of daydreaming about Mary. I wasn't getting sexually aroused if that's what you're thinking.

Anyway, when I thought about Mary, it wasn't like that. I was just looking for help and for someone to listen to me. So as Saturday arrived, I was excited about meeting up with her again.

Chapter Ten

When I first noticed her entering the bar, I thought she walked with a very slight limp but she seemed happy enough and noticing me, motioned towards the upper chambers. I patted Ralph and followed her into the room.

"How have you been? You've been on my mind quite a bit this week." I don't know why I said that. It sounded like a pick up line. And I was paying her for her time. So why did I have to worry about it? Anyway it was true.

"I've been fine," she said as we settled into the room. It wasn't much of a room, very plain. It had a pullout sofa, a couple of lamps, a side table and a hot plate. Really, it was just a room for Jake when he wanted to stay over. Obviously, it was a room for Mary too.

"What do you mean I've been on your mind?"

I wanted to say, "what do you mean what do I mean? Can't you understand English?" But I didn't want to hurt her feelings so I said, "well, I don't know Mary. I guess I kind of thought that we made a connection last week. That's all."

"What makes you say that?"

"Well, I have a feeling you could be a good listener and I guess that's all I need right now."

"Do you want a cup of coffee?"

"Sure, thanks."

Already there was a change from last week. Remember she started taking her clothes off? This time she was making a coffee for me. I think she was thinking about me too.

"Do you mind if I ask you where you came from, Mary?"

"What do you mean? Before I came to Toronto?"

"You mean you're not from Toronto?"

"No, I came here from Vancouver."

"How long have you been in Toronto?"

"For about six months, I guess."

"And how did you find Jake's?"

"You ask a lot of questions, don't you?" She said this not in a way that made me think she was upset but just as one making an observation.

"Well, I used to know Jake's big brother in Vancouver. He owns a bar out there, too."

"Jake has a bigger brother?" This was amazing as Jake himself was easily six foot four and weighed close to three hundred pounds.

"Yes, they're like brothers to me. Billy, Jake's brother, when he found out I was coming to Toronto, gave me Jake's address and when I got here, I looked him up."

"That's wild. Why did you come here in the first place? Did you not like it in Vancouver?"

"It was okay but I just thought a change of scenery would be good for me. Besides, I like travelling." Mary gave me my coffee after asking me how I liked it. I sensed a real kindness in her.

"Now let's talk about you. After all, that's what you're paying me for, isn't it?"

"Well, I guess so."

"What do you mean?"

"I thought we were sort of getting to be friends."

"And your point is?"

"Well, you bring up the money part and it makes me feel kind of sleazy, you know." She sort of grimaced.

"Oh, don't get me wrong. I'm going to pay you. I was just starting to think of you more like a friend."

Then right out of the blue, do you want to know what she said to me?

She said, "you've been buggered, haven't you?"

"How did you know?"

"Well, you hire a prostitute, someone you don't even know and all you want to do is talk. You tell me you can't talk with your parents and you don't have any friends you can confide in. You don't have to be a shrink to put two and two together."

Mary was one of the best things that ever happened to me. I couldn't believe that anyone could be as insightful and intuitive as she was. Not only that but she was beginning to show an interest in me that no one else ever had. But when you think about it, people who have things in common so often find one another. I suppose that's why I sought her help in the first place.

"I don't know what to say, Mary."

"It's true, isn't it?"

"Yes, it's true."

Then after a long pause, just staring at my coffee cup, she touched my hand and said, "tell me about it."

Then I just blurted it out.

"A priest screwed me when I was twelve years old."

Immediately, there was a change in her facial expression. Hard to explain how her facial features changed all of a sudden. You could tell that she wanted to listen to my story. At least that's what I thought until she said,

"How does that make you any different from half of the people I know?"

"What do you mean?"

"Why do you think any of us do what we're doing?"

"You mean the same thing happened to you too?"

"Sure. My grandfather screwed me when I was six years old and he kept it up for years. He told me I could never say anything to anybody or he would get angry with me. He said no one would ever believe me anyway."

"And you never told anyone?"

"No, just some friends I met here on the street."

It's what I've always said. People seek out the common denominator. They look for people just like them. That's why Mary recognized me as being abused.

"But why did you become a prostitute?"

"I ran away from home when I was fourteen and I've been on the road ever since. At first, I just slept in the parks and took scraps from wherever I could - alleyways where the restaurants dump out their garbage, stuff like that. Then some guy spotted me one day and asked me if I wanted to make some easy money. So, I said I was game for anything. He told me I could make a bundle on the street by being a prostitute and he knew how to get me started."

"Was he a pimp or something?"

"No, he was a guy just like you. He was making his living on the street."

"You mean he was a prostitute too?"

"That's right. So anyway that's how I got started and I haven't stopped since."

"Did you ever want to stop?"

"Sure I did and I will too, just a couple of more years and I will have enough dough to go legit. But what about you? What's your story? God, I told you I didn't want to talk about me."

I could see she didn't really want to talk about herself anymore and I could understand why. I was forcing her to think about her past.

"A priest? God."

"Yeah, I always thought he was a pretty good guy. We used to play floor hockey in the church basement and he asked me to stay one night after the game and that's when it happened."

"You mean it happened once?"

"No, it happened a lot of times after that."

"What did he do?"

"I don't want to talk about it, if you really want to know."

"Fine, no problem but I have to go now."

"You have to go already?"

"Yeah, what's your problem? You only paid for thirty minutes and already I gave you forty five."

"Well, can I see you again?"

"Sure, same time next week?"

"Yeah, I guess so."

"Look kid, nobody gets a free ride in this world. So you got off to a bad start. You've got your whole life ahead of you, you know what I mean?"

"God, I wish I could stay here with you a lot longer."

"Well, you can't, I've got things to do. Gotta pay the rent, you know?"

"Can't you just stay another half hour?"

"I'm going now. You better come with me or Jake will be up here checking."

"See you next week then?"

"Same time, same station."

I don't know what it was about Mary. As she walked away, I noticed her slight limp again You had to really look if you wanted to notice it. Anyway, I felt that night as if we had made a connection and I think she felt the same way. You could sort of tell. On the way out, she bent over and kissed me. I was sure that my life had been saved.

What irony! My life had been saved by a prostitute. Mary Magdalene would have been proud. But you know what? I think our talk really took a lot out of her. I figure by talking with me, she was being forced to relive her own horrors. Anyway, the next week couldn't come fast enough for me.

Now, just in case you are wondering where I was getting money to pay for Mary's services, I had a job delivering for a local drug store. I was making forty bucks a week and that included tips. I was a pretty good pool player too. I hustled every week, even played hookey a few times to hit the local hall. I always could make an extra twenty or thirty a week. Naturally, I never told my folks about these weekly escapades. They always thought I was at school.

But you know, in retrospect, I was fighting for my life here. Do you understand what I'm saying? I didn't know who to turn to for help. I sure couldn't talk with my mom about it or teachers or any of my so called friends. I was so depressed I just wanted my life to be over and I seriously considered suicide. I had a razor and really tried but I just couldn't talk myself into it. You know back then it was believed that if you committed suicide you wouldn't get to heaven. I think you know by now that my religious beliefs were and are very important to me. My mom said that God works in mysterious ways and I had no idea what She had in store for me. All I knew was that I was desperate and Mary was the first person I had ever met who seemed to understand me and what I had gone through. It was as if I was drowning and someone had thrown me a life preserver.

We used to joke around when we were kids and a common insult was calling someone a jerk or an asshole or an idiot or whatever and the favourite retort was always, "takes one to know one." There's so much truth in that flippant remark. Mary understood kids who were sexually assaulted because she had been assaulted too

You won't believe what happened next, Doc. But it's true. Out of the blue, some priest stopped me on my way out of the church on Sunday and asked if I would speak with him. I looked at him skeptically and asked him what it was about and he told me it was about Fr. Whiskers and that he had something to share with me and it would only take a few minutes of my time. So, naturally, I said okay and I met with him in the rectory office. Guess what? You're not going to believe this but honest to God, it's true. He offered me one hundred dollars in an envelope. I asked him what this was for and he said he wanted me to forget about what happened and then he asked me to sign some papers. I took the envelope and told him to stuff the papers. Then I asked him how he came to know about me and Fr. Whiskers. You know, Doc, confidentiality and all. He wouldn't tell me but said I was going to regret not signing the papers.

He said that a good Catholic would try to understand and forgive. Can you believe that bullshit? Like, because I was a Catholic, it was my duty to believe him just because he was a priest. God's representative on earth, remember? I said "how about how I've felt all this time? Doesn't that count for anything?" He said that Fr. Whiskers was going through a really hard time when he took advantage of me and I said what do you mean and he said that his mother had just died and he was in really bad shape and that I should forgive him because that's what our religion was all about. Then I said, "so he lost his mother. He's an adult for God's sake. I lost my father when I was only five. Have

I been picking on little kids?" Anyway, I started to feel that twinge of Catholic guilt again and I couldn't help it so I told him I would forget about what happened between me and Fr. Whiskers and I wouldn't say anything to anyone, not that I intended to anyway, because I didn't want anyone to know about it. But I never did sign his goddamn papers and I was happy because at least I had an extra hundred dollars and that meant I could see Mary a few more times without worrying about the money.

Anyway, that guilt trip gets me every time as I still felt a little guilty. That's why I always say to new Catholics that they're lucky because they haven't been brainwashed like I was, being born into the faith and all, and they don't have the guilt that goes along with being a Catholic, born and raised, and that they will make better Catholics than a born Catholic could make any day.

Now you probably want to know how that priest knew about Fr. Whiskers. After all, I'm sure you know, priests are not allowed to divulge information on any of the confessions they hear. How should I know how he knew but I can guess. Maybe the heat was on the Catholic church because of other child abuse sex scandals. Remember, this was long before Mount Cashel made the news, although it probably took place around the same time. But I bet the clergy was alive with rumours. Don't forget, every one of the priests had another priest to hear his confession. I think Fr. Whiskers had a confessor who couldn't take it any longer. He probably ended up talking with his bishop or something. Imagine what he had to listen to. Every time he gave absolution he would probably pray that he had sinned for the last time. But time and time again his confessor heard the same sin. "I buggered a kid or I molested a young boy or I can't get these

101

thoughts out of my mind or I can't help myself." Imagine the anguish he must have gone through, not Fr. Whiskers but his confessor. That's what I think happened anyway.

I could hardly wait to see Mary again. I mean, yes, she was attractive for sure, but that wasn't my reason for going to see her, Doc. For the first time in a long time, probably since I was abused, I had someone to talk to about it. I can't really describe how happy that made me feel. Maybe the only other time I felt that happy was the first time I went to confession and told the priest that I was satisfying myself a little too often, if you know what I mean, and he told me that it was natural but that God didn't really want us to do that but that He would always forgive and asked if I would say ten Hail Mary's for my penance and then he gave me absolution. That was the first time I ever confessed to the sin of self gratification but when I left the confessional I was on cloud nine. Some would say I was full of the Holy Spirit. I felt like singing and I'm sure I couldn't wipe the smile off my face. I was fifteen at the time. Well, that was the same feeling I had about going to see Mary.

The days couldn't pass fast enough. I even put on a spurt in the classroom and the teachers noticed that I was giving a better effort and they were pleased. They didn't see me like this very often.

You know, Doc, I really enjoy being here with you and I do feel better getting all this out. I don't know how you can stand it though, listening to nothing but problems all day long. Anyway, thanks.

Chapter Eleven

I arrived at the bar a little earlier than usual, nodded to Jake the owner and sat in my usual seat at the back of the bar. There were a few people there already and one of them was pretty drunk. I hoped that he wouldn't notice me but unfortunately he did. He made his way over to my table, stumbling against a chair and another table and knocking over two or three glasses that shattered on the floor. Fortunately for me, Jake noticed him and told him to clear out. He cursed at him for being so clumsy and then asked his maintenance man to clean up the mess. I swear to God, this kid came out who was no older than me and he had a pail and a mop and he wiped up the floor and picked up all the broken glass.

I said hi to him and he nodded back. I said that he didn't look old enough to be working in a bar and he said he wasn't but that Jake was a good guy and he hired him to do a few hours a week maintenance. He said he was in high school just like me and he could use the few extra bucks that he brought home and gave to his mother. They were living in the government sponsored housing development not far from the bar. He had two younger brothers and a younger sister at home and his mother worked twelve hours a day to keep the family going so he worked as much as he could to help out. His name was Gerry. He was well built for a kid his age, a nice looking kid too. I said that I hoped to see him again and he said if I kept coming in here I would see him again. He said he wouldn't mind talking with me a little more but he had more work to do. Besides, Jake was giving him the eye so he had to get going. Well, no sooner had he left when Mary came through the door. She looked great as usual and I was relieved and happy to see her. She nodded to Jake and he motioned in my direction. She caught sight of me and made her way to my table.

"So you're back again, eh?"

"Well, yeah. Did you think I wasn't going to come?"

"I wasn't sure, you know. You're just a kid. Not too many kids come in here."

"I'm hardly just a kid. I'm seventeen years old. How old are you anyway? I bet you're not that much older than me."

"It's impolite to ask a lady how old she is. Anyway, do you want to go upstairs?"

"Sure, I do."

"You have any money with you?"

"Sure, no problem. I'm loaded."

"Where do you get all your money anyway?"

"You won't believe what happened to me this week."

"Did you win a lottery or something?"

"No, but I did come into a little money."

"Let's go upstairs to talk about this."

I patted Ralph on the way by and this time he hardly looked at me. Just a wag of the tail told me he recognized me. That's another thing about dogs. Once they get to know you, that knowledge is locked right in. It's always better to be nice to dogs. Why wouldn't you anyway?

We sat down on either side of the small table.

"Last time you told me about your childhood and what your grandfather did to you."

"Yeah and I also told you that it is fairly common, at least with the people I know."

"Well, I don't know anybody who's been taken advantage of sexually before so that's why I like to talk with you."

"When I came in, I saw you talking with Gerry. He's one of us too."

"You're kidding. Man, he's a well built guy too."

"What's that got to do with anything? He works out with the weights all the time."

"Well, I was just thinking that he looks like he could take good care of himself."

"So do you. What's that got to do with anything? You know you haven't told me much about yourself yet."

"I told you what happened to me."

"Oh yeah, you said you were screwed by a priest. I think that's what you said. Are you still going to church on Sundays?"

"Yeah I still go."

"A lot of people would just stop going. I know I did."

"What do you mean? Are you a Catholic too?"

"A recovering Catholic."

"What does that mean?"

"I think there's too much hypocrisy in the church, you know."

"You mean with the priests and what they do."

"Right. I don't feel like going to church and receiving holy communion from some priest who's just come out of a church basement where he's been fooling around with a young kid like you."

"I guess a lot of people feel that way. But I just have this feeling that the priests are human and they don't have anything to do with my relationship with God. I mean, that part will never change. Besides, you can't paint them all with the same brush."

"Well, I have a relationship with God too and I know He looks out for me."

"I always think that God is a she you know because I think women are more loving and more nurturing than men are."

"That's ridiculous. You don't think men can be loving and nurturing? "

"Well, I've never seen it."

"Do you have a father?"

"No, he died when I was five. I had a stepfather but I never really got too close to him."

"Well, don't you see that's why you think God is a woman? You've just had your mother around. You've had no male influence except with a Catholic priest and when that didn't work out, you figured that men were just bad."

"Yeah, maybe but anyway, how long do I carry this guilt around with me? I somehow feel that I had something to do with the relationship. I mean I kept going back."

"Did you love him?"

"I thought I did you know. I thought he was taking care of me. I mean he was supposed to be God's representative on earth."

"Oh, not that shit again. Do you really think God would go around fingering all the altar boys in a church basement? No way, you just ran into the wrong man, a bad man and one not worthy to be a priest."

"Mary, why don't you give up being a prostitute?"

"I told you I would give it up in another year or so when I have enough dough to go legit."

"You just seem so smart, too smart to be hanging around here. Don't you think it's kind of dangerous sometimes?"

"Yeah, I guess so. You do meet some real creeps but where else can I make this kind of money?"

"I just think you could do real well. You could become a shrink you know. I like the way you talk to me and you listen real good too."

"Well thanks, maybe I will be a shrink some day but right now I'm working and it's time for me to go."

"Can I see you again next week?"

"Same time, same station."

I felt so much better after talking with Mary. What irony! She was a recovering Catholic, Mary the prostitute, just like Mary Magdalene.

The next week went well. I studied and did very well on school tests and I could tell my teachers were pleasantly surprised. And if you want to know the truth, I felt very good about myself for the first time in ages. Even my mom noticed a big change. We talked and we laughed together for the first time in a long while. I even sat down with her at the piano and we sang. This was a good time for me. Mom didn't mind me drinking at home but cautioned me against overdoing it. The fact is I enjoyed drinking. Maybe it gave me false courage. Maybe it helped me open up to people I thought I could trust. I mean it wasn't until later in my life that I learned that other drunks would think that what they were saying was important or funny but it really wasn't. Mostly, it was just rambling nonsense from a wet brain. But I continued my prayers and still felt I had a good relationship with God. I really felt She was listening to me and was watching over me. In my down times, times when I even thought about suicide, She saved me. I would pray to her and say if you get me through this I will live for you. Just get me through to my twenty first birthday and then I will be able to handle my life so much better. Funny thing, I used to think that when I reached the age of twenty one, I would be an adult and then magically, as if overnight, I would find the strength to battle my demons and I would win. I know now that wasn't true but at the time, it did save me, holding on to that little thought.

Mary Magdalene. Now's there's somebody I definitely have to meet when I get to Heaven. I mean she was the one who was there with Jesus when he died. She was the one who washed his feet. I think she really loved him and knew who he was but he was a man too and I bet he loved her. Maybe he felt about her the way I felt about my Mary. I don't mean I'm like Jesus in any way. Well, maybe in a way. We were both human and I guess that means that we both had feeling below the waist and in our hearts. I wonder if there were pedophiles in Jesus' day. I'm sure there must have been. I wonder if anyone ever looked at Jesus in that way, you know, some perverted Roman who had to feel important by picking on some little kid. I'm betting no one would ever have had the nerve to approach Jesus in that way because he was the Son of God after all. His mother Mary knew that because she was told that she was going to give birth to the son of God. If that didn't give you confidence, nothing would.

Doc, I know that I'm not the first person in the world this has ever happened to. It's been going on for ages and will continue long after I'm gone. Some atheists would likely say that this is proof that there is no God because He would never let anything like this happen, especially to a kid. But I believe in free will, you know. God doesn't boss us around all the time. He lets us make up our own minds. Sometimes I wish he wouldn't but that's just the way it is. I really think we have to earn our way into Heaven.

Anyway, I was beginning to understand that sharing intimacy with another didn't always mean sex. I think I shared an intimacy with Mary and she made it a beautiful experience because she listened. If sharing an intimacy with another meant that you were in love with that person, then I guess I was in love with Mary. I wonder if Jesus felt the same way about Mary Magdalene. What intimacies did they share? Do you think he would have said, "Mary, it's not easy being me, the son of God. I'm supposed to be pure of mind and body, perfect in every way but as long as I am a human being, I'm not going to be perfect. It's only when I return to my Father that I will achieve perfection." Wow! What an intimacy. And to think that Jesus would have shared this with Mary. I bet he did.

Ken Hills

Chapter Twelve

I continued to visit Mary every Saturday afternoon in the same place. I was beginning to be a regular at the pub and I began to learn a little more about the patrons. Of course, Jake was the owner. He was over six feet in height, I think I told you, six feet four inches actually and, honest to God, he had to weigh three hundred pounds. They say his brother was even bigger, at least six foot six. Anyway, the thing is Jake had a head that was shaped like an egg, that is, long on the side and more pointed on the front. He looked like he was in pretty good shape too with the kind of body that was very athletic. He had very strong features and curly brown hair. All I know is I sure would like to have him as a friend. Anyway, as Mary told me, Jake's older brother operated a pub out there in Vancouver and he phoned Jake and told him about Mary. Mary was just a street kid out there and Jake's brother took her in and sort of watched out for her. So when she came East, he phoned Jake and told him about her and asked him to please keep an eye on her.

Anyway, Doc, Jake wore false teeth. I knew this because one evening I saw him get into the middle of a fight. Two locals, I supposed, but not regulars, were going at it when Jake tried to break it up. One of the guys inadvertently knocked Jake's teeth out. Both patrons were swiftly dispatched from the bar. That's how I knew his teeth were false. I know that probably doesn't mean much to you but I always associated people with false teeth with having a rough life, like one of my students, George.

George was a sixteen year old toughie who lived in a modest bungalow with his ten brothers and sisters. He had only a few teeth that he could call his own and he looked like and was an aggressive kid. You see, George was a fighter and he often took the law into his own hands. He wasn't a bully, however. He had a heart. If a younger kid was ever seen to be picked on by a senior, the older one would have to answer to George. I remember one day, in a Business Practice class in grade nine, I asked the class if anyone could tell me anything about cheques. George politely put up his hand and obligingly drew a cheque on the board, explaining as he did so his knowledge of cheques. When I asked where he obtained this knowledge, he replied that he had learned everything from his brother who was serving time in the Guelph prison for forging them. George was always very helpful in class.

There I go again, rambling. Anyway, the regulars never fought in Jake's bar. They had too much respect for the owner and besides they considered this their meeting place and took pride in coming into the pub, a home away from home. Sort of like the way Tim Horton's is now, you know what I mean? I always see groups of people in there, sitting together, sharing a coffee and telling their stories to anyone who will listen. In fact, those restaurants are like shrink factories, if you ask me. How many stories have been told in there?

Gerry was the one who interested me though. He was my age and appeared to be a hard working guy. As I said, he was helping out his mom and trying to stay in school. One evening I arrived a little early for my appointment with Dr. Mary - that's what I started to call her - and Gerry was there cleaning up as usual. He asked if I wanted to join him for a cup of coffee in the back where Jake had a bit of a kitchen. He didn't sell coffee to his customers but made sure they had one if he thought they had too much to drink and were unable to make their way home. That's the kind of guy he was, very thoughtful and very sensitive to the needs of others. Anyway, Gerry poured me a cup of coffee and started a conversation by asking me a few questions.

"How long have you been coming here now?"

"Every Thursday for three months."

"You like Mary a lot don't you?"

"Yes I do. I call her Dr. Mary now. She's been very good to me."

"Why do you call her Dr. Mary? She's not a doctor. She's a prostitute."

I didn't like Gerry calling her a prostitute. That was too demeaning. To me, she was more important and she was helping me more than any doctor probably could.

"To me she will always be Dr. Mary."

"Do you still go to school?"

"Yeah, sure, why not, don't you?"

"Yeah, why?"

"I don't know. You seem to work pretty hard in here."

"I like to help out at home. Besides, I can use a little spending money."

"What grade are you in?"

"Twelve."

"Same as me. What are your favourite subjects?"

"I don't know, Math I guess. I like figuring out problems. What about you?"

"I enjoy reading a lot. Math is okay but I prefer reading."

"Do you have a favourite book?"

"Yeah, Catcher in the Rye by J. D. Salinger. Ever read it?"

"Yeah, as a matter of fact I have. That Holden Caulfield is quite the character."

"Do you like him?"

"Well, I don't know, sort of I guess. But I think he's a bit of a hypocrite."

"What do you mean?"

"Well, he says he doesn't like phonies but he's one himself."

"Yeah I guess so but I think he's just trying to survive and if you're just trying to survive you'll do anything, even lie to people, you know what I mean?"

"I know all about how to survive. If you live where I live you need to learn fast."

"Why? What's wrong with where you live?"

"You should come over and visit us sometime and I'll show you. Don't you have any other friends? I mean how come you come here all the time?"

"I don't come here all the time, just once a week. Yeah, I have other friends, some guys from school. We play ball together, you know football and basketball. So, yeah, I hang out with other guys too."

"Well, what do you do besides play sports with them? I mean do you go to dances and stuff like that?"

"Sure, I go to sock hops at the school."

"Do you have a girlfriend?"

"Gerry, how come you're asking me all these questions, man? How about you? Do you have a girlfriend or do you have other friends?"

"No, I don't have a girlfriend. I don't have time for that right now. Oh, I know a few girls at the school but I never asked them out for a date or anything like that. Anyway, it's good talking with you. Maybe we can do this again sometime."

"Sure, why not?"

Gerry had to get back to work. He seemed friendly enough to me but I couldn't imagine what kind of home he had or what his life was really like. That's the thing when you meet people in a bar. You never know where they live and you haven't a clue about their home life or their life away from the pub. So, in a way, I guess the pub is kind of a leveller. Maybe that's why the people who go there all the time like going there. They don't have to impress anyone with their possessions. Probably most of them don't have much anyway. The fact is, though, a pub is sort of a refuge from the rest of the world. Granted, it's not always a safe refuge but it can serve as a bit of an escape from reality for a while.

Still, every once in a while, the outside world does creep into a pub. Someone who maybe has had a bad day, is in a bad mood, may try to take it out on someone else. That's another thing I noticed. It's like being part of a pyramid sometimes, you know what I mean? If you are on the outside world and someone sits higher on the pyramid than you do and looks down on you and then exerts his or her power over you, you can go into a pub and find someone who is lower on the pyramid than you are and you can take out your frustrations on that person. They say that the cream always rises to the top. Well, if that is true, then shit always comes down to the bottom and touches anyone in the way. At least that's the way I see it anyway.

Maybe that helps to explain Fr. Whiskers. Who knows? Maybe he didn't see eye to eye with the Bishop. So whenever he had a chance he took it out on the kids. Don't get me wrong. I'm not trying to make excuses for the son of a bitch. But I learned in Physics class one day that for every action there was a reaction. I guess I'm living proof of that. In fact, who isn't? Everyone has a story. It's just that some are a little more dramatic than others. In any case, the fact is though, that with Jake and Gerry and Dr. Mary, I started to feel part of an understanding and supportive family. I know now that I sort of omitted my own family from the picture and I know they would have been so supportive but you know something, I'm glad I never involved them, especially my mom. I really think it would have killed her. God's representative on earth, remember?

Jake never asked me about myself but he was as cool as a cucumber, whatever that means. Cliches man, they really slay me. Athletes always say things like one day at a time. Come to think of it recovering alcoholics say that too. I suppose cliches have their place. Anyway, whenever I talked with Jake, he would say nothing about himself but he certainly was interested in hearing the stories of the other patrons. Don't get me wrong. He wasn't a snoop or anything like that. He was simply a good listener. Gerry told me a bit about Jake. He said that he was from a small village in Newfoundland, a rugged kind of a guy who left that province with his brother because they couldn't see much of a future there for themselves. They both loved to fish and came from a long line of fishermen but they just couldn't see themselves doing that for the rest of their lives. They heard the other fishermen in their village talk about the cod stock and how it seemed to be diminishing. Their grandfather could remember how easy it used to be to catch the cod but that seemed to be changing.

Like most Newfies, they were both just naturally friendly. In Jake's case, if he were pressed to talk about himself, he would only talk about Newfoundland and how he missed it and that someday he would go back home.

Have you ever noticed that about Newfies? No matter how long they are away from the province, it is always referred to as home. And they all want to go back there. Who doesn't want to go back home? Home is such an interesting word to me. When we were kids, we played hide and go seek and if you were spotted but made it "home" first, you were safe. There's nothing like making it "home" safe in a baseball game as it meant you scored a run for your team. Sometimes you hear that "home is where the heart is." So who doesn't want to go home and be safe where people love you?

Anyway, Jake apparently came to Ontario as a young man and worked at various jobs but it was the pub business that appealed to him the most. With what money he had, he started a modest pub. Actually, it was in an old downtown house on a large piece of land but Jake was the handiest person I ever met. He could do everything. So, over the years, he added a huge addition to his house with the help of his Newfie friends. And so the pub became known as Jake's house. There was a plaque that was hung over the bar. It read: Jake's House, built by Jake and his friends, John, Billy and Herman, 1951.

I already told you that Jake's House was like a home away from home for so many. It wasn't exactly for Newfies only but it always amazes me how they will find one another. Jake was loved by all of his patrons and he treated everyone with respect. But those who knew him knew that they didn't dare get on his wrong side. Jake had a way of dispensing justice swiftly and effectively. The music in his bar was mostly down home music. He said it reminded him of his roots. He lived in this big Ontario city but his native Newfoundland lived in his heart.

Anyway, I had arranged to visit Gerry at his place the next afternoon. It was a Saturday and I was usually out of the house somewhere doing something. And speaking of home, aren't most people like that? I mean isn't Robert Frost correct when he says that "home is where, when you go there, they have to take you in?" It's a base and a place for you to have shelter and food, a place where you keep your clothes and any other special articles that you might cherish, like the scapular medal my mom gave me for my confirmation or my Beehive hockey cards or my allies. I know, I'm a little bit old for that kind of stuff now but some things are special for different reasons. I mean all of these keepsakes reminded me of a happier time in my life. Why would I get rid of them? Sorry, Doc, I do seem to get carried away, don't I? Anyway, what I'm trying to say is that I wouldn't really be missed around the home on a Saturday afternoon so it was a good time for me to visit Gerry.

Chapter Thirteen

I took the streetcar downtown and walked over from Yonge Street to where Gerry lived. Actually, I didn't realize he lived so far away from the main artery but I was in no hurry and sort of enjoyed the walk through that part of the city. Actually, anyone who knew me always said that I was never in a hurry for anything. My mom used to tell me that some day I'd be late for my own funeral. I was becoming more and more comfortable being alone but felt good when vendors out sprinkling their produce for Saturday shoppers would stop and nod or say hello. It's nice, you know, when strangers say hi to you on the streets. I know you're always told not to talk to strangers. But it's sort of nice to be friendly to someone you don't even know, especially since you don't have to stop and hear their stories. And, no doubt, everyone had a story.

Gerry didn't live too far from the ravine. His area definitely had the look of government housing. Oh, there were playgrounds but half the swings were missing and graffiti was painted on the slides.

Now that's the very thing that would drive Holden nuts, Doc. He always wanted to protect the kids and he wanted to erase all the "fucks" and the "for a good time" writings from the side of buildings or on park benches. If he could do anything besides freezing children in their pre teen years, making them stand still forever, he would have every bit of graffiti erased from wherever it appeared. You've heard of divine intervention. Well, this was human intervention, the kind of thing that seemed unstoppable. I mean what kind of a chance does a kid have to grow up and lead a normal life when just about the first word he learns is fuck? It has to have an effect, don't you think?

Well, anyway, besides the graffiti, there was garbage strewn over the playground and papers clinging to the side of the tenement housing, blown there by the wind and plastered on by the driving rain of the night before. There were syringes and condoms, the flotsam and jetsam of a downtrodden and impoverished living quarter. This place was a haven for rats and mice. Gerry even told me that there were rats in his place.

When I knocked on his door, he was quick to answer. He opened the door and I caught a glimpse of the inside of his dwelling. It was one of those snapshot images that sticks with you a long time. There was his little brother, probably no more than five, sitting in the middle of the room, snot running down his smudged face, playing with a fire truck that had no wheels. His sister, probably just a few years younger than Gerry, sat on a sofa that had a big tear in the back of it, as she watched her little brother. She looked up with glazed and curious eyes, like she had never seen anyone enter her corner of the world before.

Gerry's mother wasn't home. She was waitressing. Gerry's dad, like Amanda's in Williams' The Glass Menagerie who worked for the telephone company, was another derelict father who fell in love with long distances and had long since abandoned his family. He left all right but not before he left his mark on Gerry. After staggering home drunk, he would beat his son, sort of like that pyramid thing I mentioned. There's always someone below you that you can shit on if you want to.

Now, it was like the whole weight of raising the family and being responsible for them rested on Gerry's broad shoulders. He saw that his brother and sister ate what food could be provided. He saw that they were in bed at night and protected them from the outside world. He saw that they were scrubbed and cleaned up for school in the morning. He took me into his room that he shared with his little brother and I saw the weights that he used every day tucked under the bunk bed. He showed me a hole in his window that looked out on to an alleyway that ran the length of the whole block. The hole was from a stray bullet that embedded in his wall behind his bed.

We sat and talked for a while, occasionally being interrupted by his little brother who wanted to come in to see Gerry's new friend. His sister called out and asked if she could go over to her girlfriend's for a visit and Gerry said okay, "as long as you're back before mom comes home because you have to help me make supper and you know what she's like when she comes home after work and there's no tea on the stove or there's no soup ready." And his sister said "okay" and I heard the door slam.

When I heard scratching coming from the wall, Gerry said "don't worry. It's only the rats moving around" and that you got used to them after a while. The whole time Gerry smiled. That was one thing about him. Here he was in the middle of an impossible situation, not of his own doing, and he smiled. It seemed that every time I saw him he was smiling. He showed me his books. He loved to read. In school he was reading Macbeth with his grade twelve class. Most of the class hated Shakespeare. It was so far removed from their own world. But Gerry loved the sound of the language. Not only that but he could identify with Macbeth in a way, certainly with his ambition to improve his station in life because in a way it was no different than Gerry, except Gerry had no one to push him like Macbeth's wife. What he did have though was some kind of force pushing him from the inside. He knew that he could be someone some day and it was that thought that kept him alive, and working day after day even here in this godforsaken run down tenement dwelling with rats scratching the walls from the inside.

We talked a little more about Holden and I asked him what Holden would think of the playground in his neighbourhood that I passed through and he agreed that it would cause him great emotional distress. He agreed that Holden would want to get out there with a scrub brush and clean up the place. Then he told me that he had his own plan for cleaning up the place.

Gerry was a painter, Doc, and a talented one at that. In fact, at the request of his principal, he had painted a huge griffin on the wall of his gymnasium. The griffin was the school's mascot. He did an amazing job. He was given permission by the tenement management to paint his murals on the side of the buildings and anywhere else he saw fit. Gerry knew his neighbourhood and he also knew that once he started that other volunteer artists would come out of nowhere to help him. And he was right. Most of these people were spray painters themselves. In fact, most of the graffiti that was prevalent in areas such as this were attributed to these young artists. But now it gave all of the kids who previously spray painted graffiti an outlet for their talents and they stopped the graffiti. In fact, this new venture gave them an opportunity to express their talent and make new friends. Every day they now had something to look forward to.

Gordon Miller was a good example of what I mean. This kid was now about seventeen years old and already had a rap sheet with the local police, car theft, defacing public property. When asked why he stole cars, he said it was because his family never got to ride in them and he always wanted to see what it was like. He wasn't malicious in his thievery. He was just trying to satisfy a curiosity more than anything. So for Gordon and others like him, to be able to do something like this, well, it was special in so many ways. It not only put them on an equal playing field but elevated them in the eyes of the public.

The Young Painters, as they became known, in fact, evolved into a club of no little significance. They painted with pride. They complimented one another on their work and they experimented with their art. In fact, because of Gerry's initiative in starting this program, neighbourhood crime decreased and the painters' self esteem was given a much needed boost.

Gerry never dreamed that his painting initiative would turn into such a major project. The painting program spread throughout the city and became so popular that Gerry received official recognition from the mayor himself and from the chief of police. Imagine a seventeen year old kid who started a wildfire of community involvement and single handedly was responsible for giving the underprivileged youth of the city something they could be proud of. Even kids who didn't have the talent that the others had became part of the project. They carried supplies - the paint, rags, tarps, cleaning supplies. They came behind the painters and cleaned up after them. The city, along with the police department, were so impressed that they bought special shirts and wind breakers for all of the participants. On these, they had a swirling paint brush with the word "painters" on the back.

This cost the city a lot of money but the project, to the public, was worth every dime. It was a source of connection to the whole community. Kids who wore the jackets and shirts, and they all did in public, received further positive reinforcement from people they didn't even know. Strangers would see them on the street and thank them for their art work and tell them how it made the city look so much better. The schools were happy too because these kids were local celebrities now and their school records improved.

That's what I mean when I say that what you do to one kid can affect thousands in a good or a bad way. In Gerry's case, the pebble he dropped into the stream rippled far beyond his imagination. There's no doubt about it. Gerry was a special person.

In my case, I began to think of how Fr. Whiskers affected me and in turn how I was affecting others. In Gerry's case, the influence was a very positive one, not only for him but for the entire community, from the kids who were on the fringes of bad behaviour to the ordinary citizen.

The Young Painters affected me a lot, Doc. I continued to excel at school. I was helpful around the home. My moodiness was replaced with civility and respect for my family and for others. It was this occurrence more than anything else that turned my life around. I felt that I was at a crossroad and I had to make a choice. I could dive into the cesspool of negative behaviour, drink myself silly and end up on the streets begging for handouts. I could become, like so many other abused kids, an abuser myself. Or I could be like Gerry and try to turn a negative into a positive. This would mean that I would have to adjust my compass but I made the decision to try. My mom used to say that God works in wondrous ways. Certainly I had witnessed an example of that. I couldn't help but wonder what further wondrous ways I would witness in my life. No doubt, there would be many more.

But as I was about to learn that if you allow yourself to get too high in this life, that seems to be the time when you experience your greatest crashes. Life is definitely a roller coaster ride and I was soon to plummet to the bottom. Why is it, Doc, that just when you start to feel really happy, so often a crisis hits?

Ken Hills

Chapter Fourteen

The next time I visited the pub, Doc, I learned that Dr. Mary was leaving our city and moving to Vancouver. As excited and happy as I was when I heard about the success of The Young Painters, I plummeted in the other direction with the news of Dr. Mary. How could she do that? She was my shrink. She was the one who was saving me. What was I going to do without her? I didn't realize or learn this until years later but whenever an upset of any kind, big or small, occurred, I considered it first in relation to myself. I never thought about the trauma suffered by the other person. I know that now but I certainly did not know that at the time, especially in my younger years. Well, actually, come to think of it, I was pretty selfish for most of my life. You see, I always needed to be accepted and now Dr Mary was leaving and I felt almost a betrayal and certainly a rejection that was going to take a long time to overcome. My mom used to tell me that God never closes a door without opening a window. It seemed to me that She had just slammed the door shut and nailed the windows closed at the same time. The next week I met with Mary for the last time.

"Why do you have to go?"

"I've been thinking about it for some time now and I really need a change."

"But what about me? What am I going to do without you?"

"This isn't about you. It's about me. Besides you're old enough now to take care of yourself. You don't need me or anyone else to hold your hand."

"But what about all your friends here? What about Jake and Gerry?"

"I will miss all of you but I need to do this for me. I want you to understand that."

"Man, I never thought you'd be leaving. Am I ever going to see you again?"

"Who knows? If you come to Vancouver, you can look me up. But I want you to promise me something because I do care for you. I really do and it's going to be hard for me to leave this place and you're not making it any easier."

"I can't help it. It just seems that every time I find a real friend, something happens. It's been that way my whole life."

"You know, all you have to do is take a walk down Yonge Street and you'll see dozens of people who are worse off than you are. You should really consider yourself one of the lucky ones."

"I know that! You don't have to tell me that! That's like telling a person who worries all the time not to worry. You can't just turn it off and on like a tap. I see those other people and I thank God that it's not me out on the street begging for pennies. But it just hurts, that's all, when you lose someone you love."

"I know. I already told you that I'm going to miss you too and I will always have a special place for you in my heart."

"What is it you wanted me to promise you?"

"Go as far as you can in school. Stay in school and go as far as you can."

"Why? Why should I stay in school? It's not doing me much good right now."

"No, not right now but eventually it will pay off for you. Eventually, you're going to be something. I know that. You're special and you need to share yourself with others, whether you do that as a teacher or a writer. Who knows what you can be? But you need to stay in school as long as you can until you find out what it is you want to do with your life and then do it. Take control of your own life and don't let others tell you what you can or can't do."

"I don't think I will ever meet anyone like you again."

"I know it's hard for you right now but I also know that your life will take a lot of twists and turns and you will most certainly meet someone special like yourself. I know it. Now I've got to go. Come here and give me a hug."

I hugged Mary, not wanting to let her go. I wept as she held me back and wiped the tears from my face. She kissed me and told me that she would always love me. Then she turned and left our special meeting room.

Ken Hills

Chapter Fifteen

That was a serious crisis for me back then, Doc. I guess when you're a teenager, everything that happens to you is magnified. At least, that's the way it seemed with me anyway. I missed school the following week and was asked by my mom why I hadn't been there. I tried to explain to her that I had lost a very special friend and I really think she understood. That was the thing about my mom. She was non judgmental and she let me be me. She also knew that the very best teacher was experience and she could see that I was struggling with a very difficult lesson. She told me that she would always be there for me and if I ever wanted to talk about it or anything else, she would always be there. What else could you ask of a parent?

I did return to school eventually but not before Jake saved me once again. One afternoon I bought a small mickey of rum and consumed all of it and staggered into Jake's, making my way to my usual spot before he noticed me. He brought me a draught, asked how I was doing and that was the last thing I remembered. I passed out at the table and fell off the chair.

The next thing I knew I was in the upstair's room and Jake was applying a damp cloth to my face and forehead. He was also giving me coffee to drink. He told me he knew why I got drunk but I had to grow up. Everyone was unhappy that Mary had left but "that didn't give you a license to give up living. You have to get over it and get on with your life." I put my faith in Jake, just as I had in Mary. But he was here and she wasn't.

When I looked at the big Newfie placing the cloth on my face and offering comfort, it made me feel like someone cared about me. God's work again! She was opening a window for me. Here was a man who was truly one of God's representatives. I learned then and many times throughout my life that angels come in different sizes and genders. After a few coffees and a long shower, I was back in the land of the living. The next day I went back to school. My mantra became "stay in school and go as far as you can." Mary's words would always be with me.

I began to excel at school and became more involved with sports and the school life. I loved to play basketball and football. They both gave me a much needed outlet to release my frustrations and even my anger. On the football field, I became very aggressive, however, to the point that even in practice the others didn't like it when I threw a block at them or tackled them because I did so with an aggression I never knew I had in me. One time when a runner on one of the other teams was heading for our goal line, everyone had stopped chasing him because he was too far away. I was too actually but I ran as fast as I could until he crossed the line and then I stopped. When my coach asked me why I kept running after him even though it was obvious he was going to score, I told him because if I ever caught him I would kill him. I learned something about myself on that day that I never knew before. Deep down inside of me there was a tendency towards violence. Most of the time it never surfaced but I learned that it was there, no doubt buried alongside my relationship with Fr. Whiskers.

I continued my relationship with Jake and Gerry and saw them both at least once a week. The Young Painters' group was still going strong. Then, one day, I dropped in at Jake's and sat in my usual spot. While there, a gentleman approached me and asked if he could sit down and chat. I said he could. His name was Josh. I knew I was going to like him right away because you could tell he was a good listener. Most people, you know, are not really interested in what you have to say. I know I told you that before but most people are not good listeners because they're just too wrapped up in their own little world. You can always tell when they turn you off. Sometimes, their eyes glaze over, like they're far away. That really bugs me, more than anything. But Josh wasn't like that. He seemed genuinely interested in what I had to say. He said that he knew that I came into this bar every week and wondered because of my age (I was now eighteen years old and would be applying for university soon), why I came in here week after week. I told him that I was welcomed here and that Jake and Gerry were my friends and they were like family to me. He understood and said that I was lucky to have such caring friends. Josh looked to be about thirty five years old. He had blonde hair and a full moustache. He was well built and looked like he could take care of himself.

The Young Painters continued to be the talk of the city. Often a photograph of one of the painters, hard at work, would be seen in one of the local papers. Jake was just as proud of Gerry as I was. What I really admired about Gerry was that, even though he was getting so much publicity and getting to be a local celebrity, he never seemed to change. He still came into the bar and cleaned up and never complained. He was still very respectful, not only to Jake, but to just about anybody who crossed his path. That's just the way that he was.

I knew this other kid at my own school. He was a star basketball player. Anything he did he seemed to excel at. Not only was he good looking, he could even play the piano and sing and that went over great with the girls. But the thing was, he was so full of himself that most of the guys at the school couldn't stand him. He thought he was God's gift to women. I bet when the girls got to know him, they would have been turned off by him too. What a goof!

Anyway, Gerry was just the opposite and that's why I admired him so much. He did confide in me that the kids at his school seemed to treat him differently. Certainly the girls drooled over him. You know when you are a teenage boy, having girls trying to get your attention is the ultimate. Gerry, although he didn't always reject their advances, mostly appeared to be disinterested. And, of course, this apparent aloofness added to his mystique and caused the girls to be even more interested in him. I have to admit. I was jealous. But that didn't mean that I thought any less of my friend.

Josh and I talked any time I saw him in the bar. And we became pretty good friends too. Always in the background was Jake. Whether he was serving at the bar or cleaning glasses, I could always notice him out of the corner of my eye. One day, when it was quiet in the bar, he came over to my table and sat down.

"How are you feeling these days?"

"Fine. But I still miss Mary."

"We all do but life goes on, right? You don't have to worry about her."

"How can you say that?"

"My brother will look after her in Vancouver. How do you like the Reverend?"

"Who?"

"You know, Josh?"

"Why did you call him the Reverend?"

"Because that's what he is. He's a Reverend."

"What do you mean, like a priest or a minister or something like that?"

"That's right. Actually, he's a Roman Catholic priest."

"What are you talking about?"

"I'm telling you, he's a priest."

"I don't believe you."

"Well, he is. Actually, he's a missionary priest and he visits different places like this all around the city. It's his job. He likes to help people."

"Josh is a priest?"

"That's right. Does that change how you feel about him?"

"God, I'm having a hard time seeing him as a priest."

"Why? Because he doesn't look like a priest?"

"You might say. I mean no white collar or black suit. He doesn't even wear black shoes, for God's sake. I've never seen a priest like that before."

"You know your problem? You judge people by their appearances. You shouldn't do that."

"But I've never seen a priest who dresses like that. I mean have you?"

"What difference does it make? He's still a priest, no matter what he wears. You enjoy talking with him don't you?"

"Yeah, but..."

"But what?"

"It's just weird, that's all."

"When are you going away to school?"

"In a couple of months, why?"

"Just wondering, are you going to be okay?"

"Sure, why wouldn't I?"

"We're going to miss you around here, you know."

"Yeah, I'll miss you too but this is something I really need to do, Jake."

"You're doing the right thing, kid. You've got the grey power. Stay in school as long as you can but don't forget us."

"Funny, that's what Mary said to me."

"What? Stay in school?"

"Yeah. You know something, Jake. I really am going to miss this place. It's like a second home to me."

"Hey kid, does your mother know that you come here every week?"

"No, I don't think so."

"Well, what do you tell her when she asks where you've been?"

"I just tell her I'm out with a friend. That's not a lie, is it?"

"No kid, that's not a lie but it's not totally honest either, you know what I mean?"

"Yeah, I know but my mom is very liberal minded when it comes to me. I guess I've been spoiled but as far as she's concerned I can't do anything wrong."

"Sounds like a nice lady."

By this time, the bar's regular customers were making their presence felt, each one in turn hollering out "hey Jake, hey kid." They were all friendly, just one big happy family. I would miss this kind of atmosphere for sure.

"Got to get back to work, kid. See you later."

That was the longest conversation I ever had with Jake. With some people, it's like that. Words are often unnecessary.

It wasn't long before Josh came in. I couldn't get over the fact that he was a priest. Any time I saw him, he had a smile or was on the verge of laughter. He seemed to fit right in with the others. There was no sense of authority in his presence. He was the first priest I had met since Fr. Whiskers that I could say I really liked. I mean, you know, Doc, I used to like Fr. Whiskers but I tried not to think about him anymore. I was finding that the more I attached myself to other people, the less I had to think about those ugly days.

Oh, I was a little nervous around Josh, just because of my background but, mostly, I could see that he was truly interested in other people. He encouraged others to talk about their lives, never demanding anything from them, never trying to convert them to Catholicism. In fact, I'm sure that most of the others didn't know that he was a priest. I suppose it was curiosity more than anything that brought him to my table in the pub. After all, he probably thought, what was a young kid like me doing in a place like this. Was I related to Jake, maybe his kid brother? Maybe I was doing a special assignment for my school? Did I have a home of my own? What was my background? Sometimes when you look at someone you can see the wheels turning. To tell you the truth, sometimes it was fun not saying anything, not giving anything of your life away to others. That way you could create a mystique that would just increase the curiosity. Do you think that's being dishonest, Doc? It sort of made me feel like someone, you know what I mean? It made me feel significant, yes, that's what it was. And when I felt that way, I felt up, you know, sort of happy and positive.

Josh came into the bar and right over to my table.

"You must really like it here to keep coming week after week."

Again the long pause. They say when you are interviewing someone, you should learn to appreciate the pause. People, in conversation, are uncomfortable with the pause. I knew this. I was going to play the interview game.

"Yes, I do."

I paused. He smiled. He fidgeted slightly, shifting in his chair.

"I enjoy talking with people like you."

"Do you just talk to people in pubs or are you friendly with everyone?"

"I have been coming in here and places like this a little more often lately."

Do you see what I was trying to do? I was trying to get him to talk about himself. It's called deflection or something like that. But why am I telling you this, Doc? Anyway, now the spotlight was shifting to his chair and away from me.

You know what I think, Doc? When you are in control of a conversation, when you have the other person talking, it gives you a sense of power, you know what I mean? Any time you have control of anything, you are in a superior position. I can see where people would like that feeling.

I was enjoying this game. At the same time, I could see how the interviewer felt. I already knew how the interviewee felt. I paused some more.

"Did you know that I'm a priest."

"Really? You don't look like a priest."

"What does a priest look like?"

"Well, he usually wears a black suit and he has a white collar on and he wears black shoes. You don't wear black shoes. How come?"

"Well, at first, I did wear black shoes. In fact, I used to wear the black suit and the white collar too."

"How come you stopped doing that?"

"Well, how would it make you feel if I came into the pub here looking like a priest?"

I thought about that one and of course he was right. I'd feel damn uncomfortable with a priest in the place. I mean he would have to see the prostitute, not that there were that many in this place. Jake discouraged it. I mean he used to let Mary in here but she was special to everybody and it was more of a pub anyway.

"Yeah, I see what you mean."

"What about you?"

"What do you mean?"

"You're not a priest too are you?"

We both laughed. But you know he had a point. I mean is anyone really what they appear to be? I mean doesn't everyone wear a disguise? Sometimes I wonder what kind of a world it would be if we all took our masks off. Sometimes I think that's what the media tries to do. They try to unmask people. Look what they did with Bill Clinton. "I did not have sex with that woman." These are words that are going to follow him to his grave and beyond. We caught a glimpse of the real man. Now I'm not saying that I am as important as the President of the United States but you know what? He's human just like me and like you. It's just that the President of the United States or anyone who is in a position of power worries more about a public image because that person is always under the watchful eye of the public. Those people need masks more than anyone.

"No, I'm not a priest. Pretty young for a priest, don't you think?"

"Yes, I guess you're right. But you seem to know about priests, at least what they wear."

"Sure I do. I'm a Catholic too you know."

Damn, I gave him a piece of the puzzle and I didn't mean to.

"Really? Where are you from?"

"You know what, Josh, I really don't feel like talking about me right now."

"That's okay. I won't bug you anymore."

"You're not really bugging me and I do enjoy talking with you. I just don't want to talk about myself."

"Okay. Listen, I have to go now but maybe I'll see you here again some day?"

"Sure. Thanks for stopping by."

I thought about our conversation after he left. I don't know why I blurted out that I was a Catholic too. I mean, why do you think I did that, Doc? God's representative on earth, I guess. He seemed to fit the description as well as anyone else I had met. Well, not really. Mary was first on my list when it came to that. She really knew how to listen and there was something indefinable about her that drew me closer to her, that made me feel like opening up more and letting her in. I wanted to take down all of my masks when she was around. I wanted her to see me like I really was. Gerry and Jake were high on my list too. They were good friends. Josh was on the radar but I really didn't know him. When you get to know someone well enough that you can take off your mask, then that's trust, don't you think?

You're like that too, Doc. You make me feel very comfortable. If you don't mind my saying, you're the master of the pause and the reaffirming nods and the "yes, I see" or "I understand" or "that must have been difficult for you" kind of interviewing techniques. You very seldom ask closed questions. I mean you wouldn't say things like "you didn't like that, did you?" Instead, the questions you ask me always require longer responses. And do you know something? I always feel like I can take off my mask when I am around you. I think it's that feminine thing again too. You're nurturing by nature and I like that. But then, you might ask, why did I like Gerry and Jake? Well, I've learned over the years that everyone has a feminine side. I think they call that the anima. Isn't that what it's called, Doc? Some people say when you let the anima side rule you, if you're a male, then there must be something wrong with you. You're probably queer. But then some are very narrow in their thinking. What's wrong with showing kindness if you're a male or showing a genuine interest in others?

Anyway, that was one of the last times I was in the pub because I was almost finished my last year in high school and I had made a decision. I wasn't going to go on to university because I didn't have the money for one thing but also I was restless. I felt like getting out of the city all together. I talked it over with my mom and as usual she understood how I felt. I mean she was only seventeen when she left her home. I was eighteen now and I was leaving home. Specifically, I was heading north to Elliott Lake, a small uranium town in Northern Ontario. It would be the adventure of a lifetime.

I said my goodbyes to Gerry, wishing him luck with his painting, although I knew he would be a success. It was hard saying good bye to Jake too but he understood. After all, he had left Newfoundland as a teenager. He understood. I even said goodbye to Josh and told him that I thought he was a very nice person, even though he was a priest. He laughed but I could see that again, inadvertently, I had given him a piece of the puzzle. I told them all I would write but that's the thing about me. I say

141

things like that but I don't really mean them. It just makes other people feel better, I think. Or is it me that it makes feel better? In any case, I admit it. I am a bit of a phony. Holden would love that, wouldn't he?

"Why did you tell me about Josh?"

"I don't know, Doc. He was a nice guy and I felt like talking about him."

Granny just stared at me. That pause again.

"Well, I guess, really, it might have been my way of saying that not all priests are perverts. I don't think it's fair to paint them all with the same brush."

Chapter Sixteen

So, you'll never guess who I saw this week, Doc. My old friend, Jack, called me and invited me back to his place for a game of golf. It made me feel good that he would think of me and ask to see me again. It is a bit of a trip up to his place but to tell you the truth I enjoyed the ride by myself. It gave me time to reflect on everything and everybody and to try to make some kind of sense out of my life. I also thought about Fr. Whiskers on the way up to visit Jack. I mean there were times when I felt a lot of anger towards him but I never would have killed him. I don't believe in capital punishment, do you? Look at all those innocent people who could have been executed if our country was still supporting capital punishment. No, I think you'd have to be a bit crazy to commit murder. I mean I know my compass was knocked off kilter but I still have a lot of control over my own life and my own decisions.

Who could have hated him that much? They say that a pedophile will molest many, many young people. So, I guess it could have been any number of victims. I also know that some victims are more severely scarred than others. They will turn to alcohol or drugs to try to forget. They may have multiple sexual relationships or they may even become pedophiles themselves. If they become obsessed with their initial tormentor, who knows what they might be capable of?

It was a very tranquil ride to Jack's place. The sun was out and there was a hint of a breeze. Since it was the middle of the week, there were fewer cars on the road, certainly not as many as there would have been on a weekend. This route was the most popular one for cottagers. I passed by the deer farm again but didn't see the dog this time. I wondered what he was up to. Isn't it strange how sometimes we think we are the only ones alive? I mean here I was driving up this highway and not even giving a thought to the millions of others on our planet. So many people doing so many things at this precise moment in time. Going to work, coming home from work, struggling for survival in a third world country, hiding from the police, creating, making love, committing crimes. I thought about our golf game and how that would go and then I thought about the great golfer Sam Snead who gave this advice to golfers who were nervous when they took their first shot, especially if others were watching. He said, "think of all those people in China who don't give a damn what happens to your ball." Smart man, that Sam. Funny how my mind flits from one thing to another, eh Doc? Anyway, we deal with our own realities, don't we? I wondered if Jack had any ulterior motives for inviting me back to his place. I would soon find out.

As I pulled on to his street once more, again he was sitting on his verandah, this time with his wife. She was a pretty lady with a small figure and a big smile. They both seemed happy to see me. I asked them how they met. Jack was a patient in the hospital, having had minor surgery and she was one of his nurses. He told her that when he was better that he would like to date her. Now they have five children and ten grandchildren. Closing doors and opening windows. There must be millions of examples of that.

After having a coffee and engaging in polite conversation, Jack and I bid farewell to his wife and made our way to the local course. Jack and I were always pretty good athletes, he more than I. We talked about playing ball together. We made a good battery, he with his fast ball and curve and me behind the plate. The day went by quickly but the game itself was secondary to our conversation. In fact, I hardly even remember playing and we didn't even keep our scores. We both seemed to be so interested in being brought up to date on one another's lives that we paid little attention to the game. Jack asked me all about my family and I asked about his. Then we reminisced about our past, about our childhood. He still couldn't believe what had happened to me even when I reminded him that he once interrogated me, shortly after my first encounter with Fr. Whiskers. He claimed not to remember that.

It's strange to me, Doc, how I can remember so many of the details around that time. I can hear the conversations and I can see the people. I can still recall vividly my times with the priest, how I struggled, how I felt. I can even feel his beard and smell his lotion. That's a memory I would love to rid myself of but I can't.

Anyway, Jack told me about his time in the seminary, five years studying to be a priest. He made many good friends in there and yet he told me he never wanted to talk about religion again. Remembering what he told me once before when we spoke, I didn't press the issue. He did confide, however, that he had recently sought counsel from a local priest but found him lacking in wisdom and too orthodox for his liking. I told him that was one of the advantages of living in a more populated locale. If I didn't like the local priest, then I could just try a different parish. I'm certain I'm not the only one who does that. Jack also told me about others from our childhood, a few with whom he still kept in touch. Each one seemed surprised to hear that Jack had no suspicions of Fr. Whiskers and his liking for young boys. He assured me that he told them nothing of me. I had the feeling that he was really checking up on me and that he really didn't believe my story.

In any case, after a long drive up there, a day out in the sun, a few drinks and no offer to stay the night, I made my way back to the city. Once again, lost in thought, not thinking about or paying attention to my speed, a policeman pulled me over and gave me a speeding ticket. Just my luck. I stopped half way for coffee and looked at the others in the restaurant. Where were they going? What were their problems? Did they have demons similar to mine? The waitress smiled pleasantly at me and I rewarded her with a small tip.

"Do you still think Jack was abused too, Doc? I mean after hearing him talk about his surprise of not knowing about Fr. Whiskers, about being in the priesthood, do you still think he was abused?"

I realized that there seemed to be no doubt in her mind. But she didn't offer any other opinion on my day with Jack. I assumed she felt that it revealed little in her understanding of me. I don't know that for sure but why else would she not say anything? I guess I wanted her to be like God, to set everything straight. Talk about unreasonable expectations. In any case, she asked me if I had given any thought to the letter she asked me to write to Fr. Whiskers. I told her I hadn't forgotten about it. Then she asked me to think more about my time in Elliott Lake and how my time there affected me.

Chapter Seventeen

Looking back on it now, Doc, I would have to say that even if my father did die before I got to know him, there were no shortage of role models in my life, positive ones too. Jake and Gerry were probably at the top of my list, Jake because of his wisdom and his strength. Gerry, even though he was the same age as me, showed me how a person can turn a negative into a positive. But then, I used to wonder, who was Gerry's role model? All I know is that he was taken advantage of also, not sexually like me but physically. I have discovered that any form of abuse leads to a negative self esteem and this can easily ruin a person. Gerry was not about to let that happen and I thought, if he could do it, so could I. Nevertheless, I looked forward to escaping from the city.

My mom cried when I left home but told me she loved me and I should write and even phone her just to let her know that I was okay. I said I would. I even had a lump in my throat but I was okay. It always gets to me a bit when I see others cry. Not long after a short ride on the subway and noticing the throngs of commuters on their way from work, coming home from work, looking for work or maybe just wanting to be out among other people, I arrived at Union Station. Again, swarms of people, coming and going, going and coming. Thinking about that now, it reminds me of a quote from E. M. Forster who once said that people spend too much time in motion and not enough time in thought. Well, I had plenty of time now for thinking as I boarded the train for the North. After finding a comfortable seat by the window, my thoughts were running in concert with the sound of the train, clickety clack, clickety clack, clickety clack. You know like someone using a metronome and playing the piano. Dr. Mary, Dr. Mary, Dr. Mary, clickety clack, clickety clack, clikety clack. Jake at the bar, Gerry cleaning the floor, mom crying, Josh the priest, clickety clack, clickety clack. It wasn't long before I nodded off and then I started to dream.

I was walking toward a cliff. The wind was howling but I heard screaming from somewhere. I strained against the rushing surf and could make out a voice that sounded like Dr. Mary's. She was yelling something about school. I couldn't make it out. Soon she was joined by others. They were all there, at least all the ones who were really important in my life. My mom was arguing with Dr. Mary. I strained to hear what she was saying but I couldn't hear her, so noisy was the crashing water against the cliff. My mom motioned me to go on. Dr. Mary motioned me to return. Gerry and Jake were waving frantically, trying to get my attention. I tried to get closer to them but each time I moved the whole picture in my mind somehow turned and they were now standing in front of the cliff. They didn't want me to come any closer. They didn't want me falling over the cliff. They were trying to protect me. All except my mom. If I wanted to continue I had to get past her. I wanted to get by her. I wanted to look over the cliff to see what was there. I wanted to jump into the raging sea. I struggled against the howling winds with the salt water smashing into my face. I made my way to my mom, the others moaning "no, no, no." But as I passed by my mom, I heard her say, "go ahead son, it's something you must do." I looked over the edge of the cliff and watched as the waves smashed into the rocks below, coming half way up the cliff. I looked back at the others and all of them, except mom, were urging me to come back.

I waved at them, turned and hurled myself over the cliff, screaming as I did so.

"Excuse me sir but are you all right?"

It was the conductor. I woke up in a sweat and assured him I was fine and that I had just had a bad dream. Aside from that disturbing dream, the ride to Sudbury was fairly uneventful but for one incident. After a few hours, the train stopped at a small station and a few people got on. They were obviously native Indians. At least it was obvious to me. They had the dark skin with long hair, two men having theirs tied in a pony tail. One of them made eye contact with me. I smiled. He didn't smile back. He had a pock marked face with dark penetrating eyes. He also had a scar that ran across his neck and up on to his chin. He was scary looking. If I were to guess at his age, I would have said that he was over fifty, pretty old anyway. What person over fifty isn't old to an eighteen year old? Anyway, they both had quite a bit to drink. It was obvious as they swayed back and forth along the aisle until they found a vacant seat. They sat. I could barely make out the backs of their heads but I could see that they were in an animated conversation about something. What happened next seemed to take place in a blur. One of them stood up and raised a shiny knife over his head. It looked like the kind of knife you could easily clean a fish with. It had a serrated edge. The other Indian raised his arms in self defence but before he could protect himself, the knife came down into him, again and again and again.

The screams and the groans pierced the silence of the sleepy car. The conductor and two burly gentlemen grabbed hold of the knife wielder, took him through to the next car while another CN employee arrived with a First Aid kit. There was blood everywhere. The attendant worked furiously applying tourniquets to the man's arms. It seemed that the damage was restricted to that area although there was much blood coming from his face as well. I don't know where the other one was taken but as long as he was away from me, I didn't care. This was nightmarish to say the least. An improbable dream was replaced with an even more unlikely knife fight.

When we arrived in Sudbury, the police and ambulance were waiting. I saw the Indian being taken into custody and the other, on a stretcher, being lifted into the ambulance. They took off into the city. It was one o'clock in the afternoon.

I knew no one in this little mining town. But I did spot the closest pub and thought I would have my pint and see what I could learn from the locals. I sat in the back of the pub with my back to the wall as usual and watched as a few people conversed in another corner and two more burly looking characters entered. One was wearing a plaid shirt with suspenders holding up blue jeans, jeans that had seen better days, worn and faded. The other was dressed in slacks and a shirt that had been recently ironed and pressed. I heard one ask the other when he was going to Elliott Lake. He said that he would be going right after he had some lunch here in the pub. I heard him encourage his friend to come with him, telling him that there was an uranium rush in Elliott Lake and there were plenty of jobs. The other wasn't interested but I seized my opportunity.

I wandered over to their table. They nodded, acknowledging me and I asked if I could sit down. "Sure," they said. I asked the neat looking guy if I could hitch a ride to the lake with him. He asked me if I was going there for a job. I said I didn't have one but I sure would like to go. He repeated that there were plenty of jobs there and I was welcome to ride with him.

I couldn't believe my luck. I bought them both a beer and they both said I looked pretty young to be buying beer. I told them I was old enough. I introduced myself and the neat guy told me his name was Harry. I think he said it was Harry Ray, at least that's what it sounded like. I told him how much I appreciated his offer for a ride and he told me to forget about it, that he was going there anyway and it would be good to have some company. It wasn't long before we were underway and I asked him a few open ended questions. I was getting pretty good at getting information this way.

I asked him what brought him to the North in the first place. He told me that he had come up from the big city, just like me. He was a land surveyor and was offered a job through his cousin, the other guy in the bar with the suspenders. He knew a guy who knew a guy. Anyway, the thing is he was just married too and his wife was going to join him in a couple of weeks. They had rented a small trailer somewhere on the lake but she couldn't come right away. He had to go because the new job was waiting for him. You could tell he missed her though and that he was excited about starting this new job. Then he asked me about myself. I told him that I had just finished high school and I heard that there were plenty of jobs up here. I told him I wanted to get away from home and try life on my own for a while. He said why don't I try getting a job where he was working. I asked him where that was and he said Milliken Lake Uranium mine. He asked me if I wanted to work in the mine. He told me that I could make tons of money there. I wasn't too fussy about working in the mines but I did work on construction in the city for the past two summers and I wouldn't mind doing that again. He was sure I would have no trouble getting a job.

After more small talk, we were silent in the car. No doubt Harry was thinking about his wife. And me, well, I was just tired, that's all. I fell asleep and this time I didn't dream. I just slept, a deep, deep sleep. I don't know for how long but what woke me was we seemed to have hit a bump and it jarred me back to consciousness. That was my first introduction to the Elliott Lake road. We headed north from highway seventeen and the road was rugged. It wasn't even paved at that time. The woods closed in on us and Harry slowed the car right down, never knowing what was around the next bend or over the next rise. Good thing too because over the next rise there were two deer, a big buck with antlers and a doe right in the middle of the road. They stared at the car like it was some strange kind of animal they had never seen before. They didn't move. Harry slowed and carefully inched his way around these two beautiful animals. They edged their way to the side of the road to make room for us and then continued grazing at the side of the road. It was the first time I had ever seen animals in the wild. I was awestruck. Never had I seen anything quite so beautiful. At the same time, I felt like an intruder. I was a long way from home.

Then at the bottom of the hill on the side of the road we saw a car in the ditch. There was no one around. It looked like the car had been abandoned. Harry drove slowly by. It was a brand new Lincoln on the side of the road. What we did notice was that the wheels were missing from the car. Other than that, it appeared to be normal looking but served as a stark contrast to the deer sighting.

The drive in from seventeen was exactly seventeen miles. Elliott Lake didn't look like much to me. At least that was my first impression. I noticed a hotel on the top of the hill, off the road a bit. Funny how I would notice that first and then an old wooden shack that had a bank sign on it at the bottom of the hill. The road was still dirt and wound its way through the town. The thing is we didn't even stop. I asked Harry where he was going and he told me that Milliken Lake was on the other side of town.

Sure enough, a few miles on the other side, there was a winding hill that led up to an old shack at the top. Harry went into the office and beckoned me to go in with him. In the office, there was a huge drafting table and two or three men were stooped over looking at some kind of drafting plan. They both had slide rules with them and appeared to be making some kind of measurements. Harry got their attention and introduced himself. Then to my surprise he introduced me as his surveying helper. One of the engineers looked at me and said he didn't remember that I was part of the deal but Harry assured him that he would need some help and that's why he brought me. After discussing this for a few moments, the engineer welcomed me and asked if I would be staying with Harry. I told him no. Well, he said then I could stay in the bunkhouse with the other workers. He took me to the door and pointed me in the direction of the bunkhouse, told me to take my things over there and when I was settled to come back and along with Harry we could have a tour of the area in the morning. Harry of course was anxious to settle in his trailer which wasn't too far away on the side of the lake.

By this time it was starting to get dark but I made it into the bunkhouse, told some guy I was working at Milliken and that the engineer had told me to come in here and get settled. He showed me to a room with a bunk bed in it. I loved bunk beds and seeing no one there, threw my bag under the bunk. It sort of reminded me of home in a way because my sisters used to sleep in a bunk bed. Anyway, I soon settled and headed on down to the mess hall for a meal. I sure was hungry. There looked to be about fifty guys in the hall. Some were just leaving but I made my way into the line and soon had a plate of steaming potatoes, carrots and chicken.

So far, my first day away from home had been filled with an array of activities that I could never have imagined. First, there was a six hour train ride up from the city, a knife attack on the train, meeting Harry, seeing my first wildlife, getting a job and having a great meal. I couldn't believe my good fortune. I said hello to a few of the workers in the hall and they seemed pleasant enough.

Then I noticed that some of them were rushing out of the hall. I asked where everyone was going and I was told that they were going outside to see the bear. Now that got my attention. I hurried out after them and stood on the long makeshift verandah overlooking the garbage dump. Sure enough, there it was, paying no attention to the curious onlookers. It just rambled out of the woods and made its way down the side of the hill into the dump. It foraged there for some time and finally, fully satisfied, it made its way back up the hill and into the woods. I asked if this was a usual event and was told that the bear visited every night about this time. I asked if there were many bears around and was told that they were there in the woods and were fairly common. I wasn't sure if I liked that idea. I was assured that if I didn't bother them, they wouldn't bother me. Just never come between the bear and its cubs.

In any case, I returned to my room, took my book out and started to write a letter. My first letter, away from home, was to my mom. I knew she would be worried although she would never let on that she was. I hardly knew where to begin and thought if the rest of my days here were anything like the first, I would be in for quite a summer. I wasn't going to be disappointed. But I also wasn't going to tell her everything that happened on my first day.

In the morning, before heading off to the shack where I was to meet Harry, I headed back to the mess hall and had a great breakfast, orange juice, eggs. toast and jam. There was plenty of food there with a beautifully equipped kitchen ready to serve the workers. Not all of the workers were miners. Some like me were working on construction gangs, clearing bush, making new roads. But all in all, in the entire Elliott Lake area, there were seven uranium mines and about two thousand hard rock miners. They came from all over the country to find work, leaving families and friends behind, eager to cash in on the uranium rush. The pay in the mines was amazing. A miner could easily make seven or eight hundred dollars a week. Remember this was 1957. Even I was making close to two hundred dollars a week for the work I was doing.

What a job! Every day I would meet Harry at the shack and then off we would go, surveying well into the bush. I would take the measuring rod and walk toward the bush until Harry told me to stop. Then I would turn, extend the rod and he would take readings. Harry was very efficient in his work and every day when we finished our job for that day we would head off to his trailer at the lake. We'd drink a beer and then run into the water to cool off. It's hard to describe how the water felt at that time. From the surface, it appeared to be almost black, sort of like the Muskoka waters but it was refreshing for sure.

In my letter to my mom, I neglected to tell her about the bear. Nor did I mention anything about my train ride to Sudbury, only to say that it was a nice ride and I saw a ton of pine trees. More than anything else, at least for me, Northern Ontario is defined by its pine trees. I didn't tell my mom about seeing the bear in our garbage dump every night either. Although she put up a good front, I know she was worried about me. I told her a bit about Harry, how nice he was and how he was the one who got me a job.

One day Harry and I were walking through the woods when we came upon a beaver dam. Nearby was the evidence of this diligent and tireless worker. Trees were felled close to the river. We looked closely at the dam and I remember thinking how talented these beavers must be. They are true engineers. Not only are they the architects of their homes, they are also the workers. Daily I was gaining more appreciation for the natural surroundings. Then I met the bear again.

We were working and Harry motioned for me to go farther into the woods. I started in when I thought I heard the breaking of twigs. I stopped in my tracks. There, probably not more than forty paces from where I stood, was a big brown bear. He was stripping a nearby wild raspberry bush. Suddenly, he stood. I could see him sniffing the air. Fortunately, I was downwind. I was told that the bear's eyesight is not the best so the best advice is to stand rigid and pretend you're a tree. That was not difficult for me, believe me. I was petrified. He continued to sniff and unable to detect any strange scents, he went back down on his fours and ambled back into the bush. In the meantime, Harry was yelling at me, trying to figure out the problem. I ran toward him and when he was within earshot, I told him what the problem was. He assured me that I would be fine and then told me if I wanted, I could bring the camp dog with me the next time.

Rusty, a German Shepherd, was good at scaring away the bear. From then on this wonderful dog was my constant companion. We hit it off right away. I've already told you how much I love dogs. They can sense how you feel about them. Rusty loved the company and he liked being out in the bush. I felt so much more secure having him along.

Harry and I hung out together until Joan arrived. Joan was his wife. They had only been married for two weeks when Harry left her for the north country. My trips to his trailer came to an abrupt halt. When she arrived, in fact, Harry, if he wasn't such a good worker, probably would have been fired if someone else had been in charge. He started to be late for work. Our work day was supposed to start at eight o'clock, and Harry started to arrive at the shack around nine, sometimes even nine thirty. The engineer seemed to understand and valuing Harry's work, he made allowances for his tardiness.

One day after work, I decided to take a walk into Elliott Lake. It was only about two miles but I thought I would just check out the town. Where do you think I would have gone first? You guessed it - the hotel. It was situated on the top of the only hill in the town just as you entered the area from the dirt road, the same dirt road that led to highway seventeen. The nearest police station was in Blind River, approximately sixty miles away. With no security, with two thousand hard rock miners, one hotel and an old makeshift wooden shack used for a bank, some would say that this was a recipe for disaster. I was soon to find out.

I climbed the hill to the bar and was surprised to find a bartender selling beer through the windows of the pub. There was a lineup to get into the pub with extra bodies surrounding the hotel but still able to buy their beer. I stood in line and waited for a spot inside the bar. At the same time, I made idle chatter with some men. There were a few who might have been around my age and, naturally, as is so often the case, like finds like. I asked them where they were working. The two I talked with told me they were at Dennison Uranium mine, a little closer to Elliot than was Milliken. After thirty minutes or so, we were finally allowed to enter the hotel. It was very plain, Doc. Jake's place back home looked like a palace compared to this. But when you think about the circumstances, it was very practical to have a plain pub. By plain, I mean wooden floors, bare walls that could use paint, old wooden chairs and tables. I thought about Gerry and how he could make improvements on the walls. In those days, you could order as many drafts as you wanted. I sat with my new friends and we ordered nine drafts. Every table was filled with empty glasses, half filled glasses and jugs of beer.

We were enjoying our beer when the first fight broke out. It was like something out of an old Western movie. Tables were tossed aside and bodies were slammed up against the wall. Chairs were used to crack heads with and glasses shattered everywhere. There were two huge bouncers who stepped in to restore order. One received a bloody nose for his trouble but together these two brutes subdued the fight. They threw the offenders out. Attendants cleaned up the mess. New old wooden tables were brought back in. The chairs that needed to be replaced were and all the glass was swept. In a matter of minutes, the pub was as good as it had been earlier which wasn't saying much. At least you would not know that a fight had taken place there only a few minutes earlier.

My friends and I resumed our chat. I found out they were in fact brothers up from the city. Both were engineering students at the big university in Toronto and came north for the experience and the money. They were getting plenty of both.

Then the second fight occurred. Well, not exactly right away but you could see it coming. This huge Indian, a strong looking man with bulging biceps, his hair in a pony tail entered the bar. He looked vaguely familiar but I thought nothing further of it. He approached the first table and we heard him say, "buy me a beer or I'll kick the shit out of you." He was invited to sit down while someone bought him a pint. He guzzled it down and went to the next table with the same impolite warning and the same result. I knew it was just a matter of time. As he came nearer, I recognized him. He reminded me of the the big Indian from the train, the same big Indian I thought was taken away by the police at the Sudbury train station. I wondered briefly how he came to be here. I must have been mistaken. I thought for sure he would be in jail. In any case, he came to our table next, and delivered the same warning. I realized that he wasn't the same Indian I saw on the train as I didn't notice a scar. We asked him to sit down and bought him a beer. He guzzled it down and went to the next table and delivered the same warning. A miner, with two front teeth missing and a knife tattooed on his right arm stood up and told the Indian to get the hell out. What happened next happened quickly. With one punch, the Indian lay on the floor unconscious. The two bouncers moved in and carried the big Indian to the front door, revived him and then told him not to come back. He made some kind of threatening remark and then left.

At six o'clock, the bar was closed and remained closed for one hour. This time was needed just to clean up the pub. The floor was swept, the tables rubbed down, glasses washed. Everything on the inside of the pub that could be cleaned was cleaned. I made my way back to the bunkhouse, having seen enough excitement for one day. Nonetheless, it was the only bar in town and so I knew it wouldn't be long before I made a return visit.

The two brothers and I walked along the road towards our camp. As we did so, we passed by five or six trailers right on the side of the road. I thought this an odd place for trailers, all the same in appearance, to be parked but thought no more of it. We walked for a mile and the two brothers turned off the main road and made their way to Dennison while I continued on up the road on my own. It seemed fairly isolated but at the same time it was still daylight and I gave no further thought to the pub.

Then I saw the bear. It crossed the road about seventy yards ahead. I thought about going back. Then I decided to follow more advice I had received about being around bears. I began to sing and made about as much noise as I could. They say unless you get between the bear and its cubs and you make lots of noise, the bear will take off. I tested the theory and it did seem to work. I was never so happy to see the bunkhouse. It had been another eventful day in the North.

Ken Hills

Chapter Eighteen

I haven't heard too much about the Fr. Whiskers' investigation, Doc. Have you? I hope they get to the bottom of it soon. I guess the Catholic church is taking a beating over this one. How can they be protected from scandal? In fact, how can any large institution that is in the public eye be protected from scandal? Power, authority, sex and huge egos make for inevitable problems, don't you think?

Anyway, back to Elliott Lake. I was invited a few times over to Harry's but not nearly as frequently as before his wife arrived. But I understood that. When I did visit, I usually had something to eat with them and then swam briefly in the lake. I was enjoying my life in the north country. One evening, composing letters first to my mom in answer to her most welcome letter, I assured her that I was fine, that there were other boys here my age. I told her that I had met some really nice people and she was not to worry about me. I also wrote to Jake and told him about the hotel and the fights. I told him I missed his pub and asked him how Gerry was doing. I asked him to say hi for me. Life went on in the camp as usual.

Looking back on it now, Doc, that summer was probably the start of my burying my sordid past. To get away from the city and all the familiar surroundings was likely the best situation for me at the time. Starting a new life in a new environment is difficult at first but I was finding that adjusting to new friends and new situations with different expectations was actually good for me. I loved Northern Ontario. I loved the wilderness, the bear, the beaver, the deer. I loved the fresh air of the North. I felt like I had left my troublesome past behind, in another world. My new world could not have cared less about my previous one. However, I learned that no matter where you go, you meet new people with problems and struggles of their own. I was beginning to feel part of the greater human family. Just as the animals of the wild were quickly adapting to the intrusion of humankind, so too were the people, the ones who sought their own means of survival. I was beginning to believe that, indeed, we are all, animal and man, just one small, insignificant piece of one great soul.

At this time I didn't realize what damage was being done to the environment. Now that I look back on it, I wish there was something I could have done to put a halt to the mining. It wasn't until years later that I learned that too many of the miners who stayed on and worked underground would later succumb to breathing problems. Some died but I guess there was no way to prove that their illness was caused by being exposed too much to the crap in the mines.

Occasionally, we would visit Sudbury for the weekend. Even there, a nocturnal visit to the slag dump at the Falconbridge mine, although exciting to see, was a precursor of pollution problems down the road. Sudbury was a wasteland at that time. There was some rumour that astronauts trained for their lunar flights there because the conditions were so moon like. Rock as far as you could see. No greenery, just rock. Years later, of course, they tried to clean up their environment so they built a giant smoke stack that solved the Sudbury problem. Within years, greenery appeared and now it has a completely altered landscape than when I was there in the fifties. Mind you, the soot and crap that comes out of their smoke stack now catches the upper breezes and comes to earth further south. Big problem, this pollution. On top of that, the lakes around Elliott now aren't as good for fishing any more and there is much less wildlife in evidence.

In any case, I cherished my time there. Walking into town to the pub, I now wore a whistle around my neck and if I was by myself, I would blow it frequently just to make sure that any wildlife in the area knew there was someone coming. And besides, I had a new friend who always watched out for me, our German shepherd, Rusty. Anytime he heard my whistle he would come running. The others didn't mind if I took him into the town with me. They could see how he had adopted me and knew as long as he was at my side, no one had to worry about my safety. So whenever I took a walk into town, all I had to do was blow my whistle and Rusty would come running.

Dogs! I already told you how I felt about dogs and if you are not a dog lover, you will never understand. Rusty and I became inseparable. He wasn't allowed to follow me into the bunk house. So he just slept outside and waited for me in the morning. I always brought him a few scraps from the kitchen. He came to work with me and was never far from my side during the day or night. He was especially helpful as we surveyed in the woods as he would wander through and if ever he saw a bear he would bark and scare it away. We heard him bark a few times and were grateful for his presence.

Then one evening, I received another shock. Rusty and I were leaving the pub and heading back to the camp when I saw her. I couldn't believe my eyes, Doc, the same almost imperceptible limp. It was Mary. There was no doubt. I called out to her.

Chapter Nineteen

We embraced like long lost lovers.

"Mary! I can't believe it! What are you doing here? It's so good to see you again. Oh my God, I thought I would never see you again."

Rusty barked with excitement and insisted on meeting my friend.

"Who's this you have with you?"

She bent and patted Rusty who returned the love by jumping up on her and licking her face. She laughed.

"You're so beautiful. What's your name?"

I told her.

"Mary, what are you doing here?"

"Me? What are you doing here?"

Well, I knew what she was doing here but I didn't know why. I thought she had gone to Vancouver.

"I had some friends who talked me into coming here with them. We're staying in the trailers by the bar."

"But why did you come here? If I were writing about this, no one would ever believe it."

"No kidding. But I'm so happy to see you. You're still in school, aren't you? Tell me you didn't quit school."

"No, I finished grade thirteen. I just wanted to take some time off, that's all. I had to get away from home and see what the big bad world was like away from the nest. I can't believe you're here."

"I'm happy to see you too. I never thought I'd ever see you again."

"Where can we go to talk, Mary?"

"Well, I don't think the trailer is a good idea right now. Maybe we can just walk."

And so we did, Mary, Rusty and myself. It was a beautiful evening and as we walked away from the town, we were both awestruck by the Northern Lights. They were putting on a light show, with shooting stars and curtains of light cascading like huge waterfalls, a sparkling, glittering spectacle. Even Rusty was impressed by the lights. She could hear the sky sounds and her head, with ears perched, tilted from side to side. I pointed to Sirius, the brightest star in the night sky. I had learned that it was called the Dog Star. Aptly named, don't you think because who could ever lose their way with a dog at their side?

Mary and I held hands and said nothing. We walked in silence along the winding, dirt road out of the town. I could feel the electricity between us and I knew she could too. We gave in. Like two long lost lovers, desperate for intimacy, we kissed, our first romantic kiss under the northern lights away from the city's glare and the drunken expletives of the Elliott Lake bar. I told her how much I loved her and she said the same. I told her I didn't want her to go away from me again and she said she wouldn't. And there, in the moonlight, in the woods, under the God filled night, we made love. It was my first time and Mary guided me. She was a wonderful teacher. As we made love, our groans were the sounds of nature and our love flowed naturally as we moved in concert with the rhythm of a star filled northern night.

"I didn't know how much you meant to me until I left you."

"I think I always knew how much you meant to me."

"I know you don't approve of what I do."

"Mary, it's just that you could do so much more with your life. You're so smart."

"I told you I would get out of this business as soon as I have enough money. And I meant it. Another year or two and I'll walk away. I promise."

"I don't want to share you with anyone else."

"With them, it's sex. With you, it's different."

She kissed me again and again I gave in. If it wasn't for Rusty whose curiosity turned to suspicious alertness, we would still have been there. There was a bear in the area and Rusty could smell it. He barked. I told Mary we had to go back. On the way back to her trailer, I explained to her how much Rusty now meant to me, how she trailed me everywhere and how she was such a wonderful guard dog. You could tell Mary was pleased. At her trailer now, she asked if I would be okay. I assured her that I would and that I had my dog to protect me. Again we kissed and I didn't want to let go of her. Reluctantly, she, being the stronger of the two, released me but not before giving me another warm embrace and another kiss. I told her I would be back again the next evening to see her. She told me to come back two nights later. I didn't think I could be away from her for that time but I said I would.

On the way home, I was floating. I danced and sang along the road and Rusty jumped happily around me. I know I was in denial about Mary and her profession, Doc, but I just didn't think about it, that's all. I just knew her to be a good person with a big heart. I really did think that I was in love with her. It was the happiest time of my life. The next day at work Harry couldn't help but notice my giddiness.

"What have you been up to?"

"What do you mean?"

"Oh, like you don't know how crazy you're acting."

"Harry, I just met someone I knew in the city."

"Well, the way that you're acting, I would have to think it was a girl."

"Yeah, it's a girl. Her name is Mary. She's very special."

"Well, I can see that. When am I going to meet her?"

"I don't know. Maybe we can arrange something."

"Why don't you bring her over to my place tonight? Introduce her to Joan and me."

"I'm going in to town to see her tomorrow night. I'll ask her what she thinks."

"Tomorrow night or any night is fine. Just let me know."

Rusty started barking again. This time Harry and I both saw the bear. It was standing on its hinds and sniffing the air, trying to figure out where we were. Its cubs were nearby. I blew my whistle loudly and Rusty continued to growl and bark. She wasn't giving an inch, even as the bear started toward her. Some of the other men from the construction crew came running. Everyone knew now that a loud whistle and barking in the area meant only one thing. They had shot guns with them, guns that they always kept in their trucks for just such emergencies. When they saw what was happening they came rushing toward us with their guns. Immediately, they began firing into the air and finally the bear stopped and with cubs in tow headed back into the woods. That was the closest encounter we had with the bear.

I couldn't help but think how we were someplace we shouldn't have been. The bear was here long before we were. This was her home and she had every right to protect it and she was big enough to do it. But who would protect the beavers and safeguard their dams, the deer of the forest, the foxes and wolves? This was their home too, just like it was the home of the Indians who lived peacefully with their forest brothers for centuries.

The Indians were an extension of the forest, of the animals who lived there and of nature itself. They saw themselves as part of nature and viewed the animals with respect. Any animal ever slain and taken for food was only done with the animal's permission. The Indians would explain to their brother, the deer or the bear, that their families were hungry and they needed them to fend off their hunger. And when they skinned and gutted the animal, they wasted nothing. They always found a way of giving the remains back to nature, leaving the guts or the inedibles in the forest where other animals could eat them.

And that was why I felt so depressed the next evening as I made my way back into town and saw that a small carnival had been set up. I saw Indians there who had come in from the woods where they had been fighting forest fires and with their money they bought booze and gambled away the rest to big city carnies who had set up shop on a makeshift midway. With promises of fancy looking gift prizes, the Indian frittered away his hard earned money and I saw a drunken Indian man, staggering and lost in a white man's world. I knew he did not understand what the white man called progress and so he gave up his dignity to the white man's greed.

Often in the local bar, an Indian would be in the centre of a fight. What rage he had! Frustrated, his natural compass thrown completely off kilter, its arrow indicators spinning, like the phony roulette wheel on the makeshift midway. He was lost and uprooted and like the bear, standing on its hinds in the forest, sniffing the air, not knowing where its intruders were, thrusting an angry paw in several directions, the Indian struck out at the unfamiliar. The natives had lived in concert with nature all of their lives. That balance was now and forever disturbed. Looking back on it, I would have to say that was the most significant example of abuse I had ever witnessed. There is no doubt that the Indian's compass had been smashed.

It was a time of change for me too. I knew intimacy for the first time as I gave over my heart to another, never knowing of the consequences, never suspecting that there would be any. Was the Great Spirit of the Indian the same as my God? Were we all just a small piece of the same big soul? I was more convinced now than ever that we were.

My mother's words came back to me. "God moves in mysterious ways, his wonders to behold. There are things in this world we will never understand. Accept them on your faith and trust that God is in control." I think my mother would have made a good Indian.

The next evening couldn't come fast enough for me. Rusty and I raced into town as soon as we could, my dog sensing my excitement and urgency. Mary was waiting for us. We walked away once again from the town, this time under the watchful eyes of the hard rock miners, no doubt wondering about the good fortune of a young city boy. Excitedly I told Mary about the events of the day before and we discussed my observations about the Indians. She listened as she always did, with obvious interest and attention. She told me that she thought I was a pantheist and I asked what that was. Her knowledge always amazed me.

"God is the universe. That's what the Indians believe and it sounds like that is what you believe too."

"Mary, I don't know what I believe. All I do know is that it makes me feel sad to see the Indian taken advantage of the way he is."

"You have a beautiful soul and some day you will make someone so happy."

"What do you mean some day?"

"You know we are both still very young. Who knows what will happen to us, where we will end up?"

"Don't talk like that. We're always going to be together."

"We will always be together because that is what we both want. Remember always that everyone we meet and get to know becomes a part of us and we a part of them."

We looked into one another's eyes. Sometimes Mary seemed so far away. I've heard of people who have a special gift, a gift that enables them to sense and feel beyond what is normal. Like a dog I think. A dog can sense something before it happens. I had a dog once, Doc, that knew when I was coming home from work or when someone was coming to the door. She would always be there to greet us. Mary was sort of like that. She could tell how you were feeling.

We stared into one another's eyes for the longest time, just looking, inviting one another into our very souls, longing for spiritual connection, not knowing that this inward journey could lead to a consummation far greater than the physical kind. Finally, we kissed again and made love under a cloudy sky with the sound of a lonely wolf, no doubt sensing eminent danger as man encroached ever farther into its territory, howling in the night.

We met most evenings for the next two weeks. I even took her to meet my friend Harry and his wife Joan. They both loved her immediately and could see why she was so important to me. What she did for a living never influenced their love for her. They just knew that she was special to me. Harry and Joan had become special friends. My life was blissful at this time but as I was to learn once again, you should always guard against being too high because you make yourself vulnerable to a crashing fall.

Chapter Twenty

When I saw that the trailers were no longer there, Doc, I panicked. I ran into the hotel and asked the owner where the girls had gone. He said he didn't know but he thought that one of them had left a letter for me. The bartender had it and gave it to me. Expecting the worst, I went outside and raced to the top of the hill that overlooked the town, tearing open the letter and I read.

"I don't know where to start. I hardly know what to say. I only know that for you to be part of my life is no longer possible. There is so much I need to tell you. I don't want to hurt you but you must learn to forget all about me. In time, maybe you will even forgive me. I know how strong you are and I also know that in time you will find your way.

When I was a little girl, my grandfather used me. He was one I loved very much and I trusted him. I thought he loved me too and I suppose in his own misdirected way he did. But he betrayed that trust just as I have done to you.

You once said that people of the same kind seek one another's company because that is where they feel most comfortable. How did you get to be so wise? That's what I have done. My friends, every one of them, have similar backgrounds to mine. We are like a giant magnet, drawing in others with similar backgrounds and problems. I won't allow this to happen to you. I don't want you to be drawn into my world. I won't allow it.

I always thought you were special from the first time I met you. I still think you are special and I'm sure that a just God has mapped out your life in a special way. Whatever you do in your lifetime, it will be with the sincerest of love and devotion. Go back to school and go as far as you can and you will be that special someone that God intended you to be. You will meet someone special, like you, someone who will accompany you in life's journey, who will guide you and understand you and love you in the truest sense of that word, in a way that I could never do.

You talked about your life's compass being tilted by what happened to you as a young boy. If that is the case, then almost everyone I know has had their compass interfered with. I know mine has. That is why I left home at such a young age, younger than you were when I first met you. You know that I took to the streets and found there many others like me. Many of them joined the same life as I have and continue to do so. Some have died along the way, falling prey to unscrupulous pimps and drug dealers. For that too is a reality of my life. I am an addict and have been for several years now. My friends are junkies and so am I. I need my drugs and I need my job to keep my drugs. Can you ever forgive me?

When I came to Elliot, I thought I could change my life. I thought that, by moving, I would somehow change and leave my old habits behind. But I learned that no matter where I go, I cannot escape my past nor be anything other than what I am. And then I met you again. We met at a time when we were both so vulnerable. And yet, it was almost as though our meeting once again was meant to be. I stopped taking the drugs, at least I cut back. But I have to confess to you that I used you. I used you as a crutch. That was what I needed and you were there for me at the right time. But my craving continued and was only suppressed slightly and temporarily by our brief affair.

It seems that everyone takes a different route through life. Sometimes our roads intersect and we don't know why they do. You would probably say that it is God's plan and we have nothing to do with that. It is hard for me to believe that you have such a strong faith, especially after what happened to you. Don't you ever get pissed off with God? Do you think He, all right She, would ever make things right again? I need to think that She will. I also think that if there is a God as you claim there is that there is a purpose to all of our lives and that some good will come of it.

You're right, you know. We are a part of all that we meet, just like the Indians who believe that we are a small part of the same big soul. Please don't hate me for using you. You are the kind of person who needs to see the best in people, the type who has that uncanny ability to turn a negative experience into a positive one. You have already had too many challenges in your life. I am sincerely sorry for giving you another one. I told you that I loved you but I don't know if I am capable of loving anyone. I say this because I have lost touch with my own reality and I'm having a lot of trouble finding it again.

I don't have the same faith as you. In fact, I really don't have much faith at all. But what I do know is that each one of us has to follow our own roads, playing the cards we have been dealt. Where those roads will lead us is anyone's guess. Don't they say that all roads lead to Rome? You would probably say that all roads lead back to God. Why do I keep using you and God in the same sentence? For now, you have turned your back on your God but you know something? When you do that, if there is a God and I'm not sure that there is, She wouldn't go away. She would just look over your shoulder. So turn around and find Her again and stay in school. Please forgive me, Mary."

I was devastated. I wanted to die. I cursed God and I cried like I had never done before. I don't remember walking back to my bunkhouse. I don't even remember Rusty being with me, so consumed was I with the letter. I read it over and over again, hoping that somehow it would read differently. I never slept that night and the first sound I heard was the barking of the dog. This usually meant that a bear was in the vicinity. But this time, Rusty was in the bunkhouse and she found me. She climbed up on to my bunk and settled at my side, resting her head on my stomach. My deep sadness was reflected in her eyes and as I silently wept, she stared with her baleful eyes, her ears pinned back and twitching slightly, ever alert for any kind of message. We lay there for a few more hours until I received yet another unannounced visitor. It was Harry.

He wanted to know what the hell was wrong with me and what was the dog doing in my room. I started to explain to him what had happened when he told me to get dressed and that I was late for work and did I want to lose my job. When I told him I didn't want to go to work that day, he pulled me out of the bed and practically dressed me, so insistent he was for me to go to work. When I told him to go to hell, he smacked me. I tried to hit him back and I missed. Then I just started to cry and he held me. He told me to snap out of it kid. The best thing I could do for myself was to get to work.

It was one of the strangest encounters I think I ever had. Normally a dog would be barking at any imminent threat to its master and in my case would have hurled himself at my tormentor. I can't explain it. All the while Rusty lay there, never taking his eyes off either one of us. I don't remember the rest of that day but as I said before, angels come in different shapes and sizes. My life has always been that way. Just when I want to jump over the cliff, someone grabs me by the scruff of the neck and hauls me back. This time it was Harry and his wife Joan. For the rest of my stay in Elliot, I stayed with them. Rusty came with me.

Joan was a tall lady with long brown hair. She always wore it in a pony tail. She was very athletic looking with a beautiful smile. I could see why Harry married her. She was very kind and while Harry could be gruff at times, she never was, and she could see right through him. He was just a loveable bear. She listened to my story and she cried along with me. And I told her everything. When Harry saw us like that, he told me to grow up and did I think that I was the only one with problems in this life? He said "you know what I do when I feel troubled? I go fishing." And then he slammed the door and headed out on to the lake. Joan told me not to mind him that he was just being Harry and that he really wanted me to be okay.

Rusty lay near Joan. He seemed to really like her and I knew when it came time for me to leave there would be a home for him. It was that female connection again.

I stayed for six weeks with Harry and Joan, Doc, drawing strength from their friendship and their kindness. And I learned something else about the loveable bear. He was a gardener. Outside of his trailer, he planted a garden, a mixture of flowers and root vegetables. Joan said he was always working in a garden, even as a young man. Where he lived in the city, it was common for a passerby to stop and view his creative work. However, once he realized that whatever he planted would soon be eaten by wildlife in the area, he stopped. He told me that they were there before he was. It was their land. They ate everything except any little plant that had a fungus on it. I found this interesting and he just explained that somehow they knew the plant was unhealthy and they wouldn't touch it. Funny thing though. Harry would clip the affected leaves and water the little plants encouraging survival. And the plants would grow and then the deer would eat them.

Anyway, I knew it was my time to leave. The Northern winds were beginning to blow and the colours had long faded from the trees. Winter was coming and I had to leave. We discussed my leaving the last few nights and they knew it was right for me to go. They both said I had to get on with my life. They were right. I wanted to leave the whole experience of Elliot Lake behind me. I wanted to forget about it. I never did but in time I learned to live with the memories. Leaving Rusty was also heart breaking for me but I knew she had a loving home with Joan. I never saw her nor Mary again.

I was still upset about Mary. Why was it that anything I ever really loved was taken from me? I thought about Gerry and the Young Painters and continued to be inspired by them. If they could survive, then so could I.

Chapter Twenty One

And so I returned to the city. I went home. My mother let me in. Sounds strange to say that, I guess, Doc, but you know, from my point of view, I wouldn't have blamed her if she had turned me away with the way I treated her over the years. But she wasn't like that. She was like the dog really. She watched and she knew that eventually I would be fine. She never said anything, never asked me to divulge any deep dark secrets. She simply trusted that I would be fine. She always allowed me to be me. I swear to God sometimes I used to think that she had a direct line to the almighty. God's representative on earth? She was first in line.

I took a job in advertising as a copywriter. I knew a guy who knew a guy and before I knew it I was called in for an interview. That was on a Friday. The manager told me, after the interview, to return on Monday to write an aptitude test to see if I had the creativity to do the job. He told me I needed to know how to type. I told him I didn't know how. He said go home and learn and come back on Monday to write the test. I borrowed my sister's typewriter and typing instructional book and started banging away on the typewriter. I typed all weekend, all day and half the night. I was determined to learn how to type. On Monday I typed the test. I started at nine in the morning and was still typing at five in the afternoon. The test should have taken no more than two hours. The manager came in and told me I was hired but pleaded with me to look at the keys when I typed from now on. I reported for work the following day.

I did return to Jake's periodically. The big Newfy was always happy to see me. When I inquired about Gerry, he told me that he won several scholarships and decided to move out West to continue his education. I had no doubt that no matter what he chose to do he would be successful. Jake told me that his brother saw Mary on occasion and that she seemed to be getting along fine. I now accepted the fact that our relationship was born out of a need to fill a craving for something else, maybe acceptance and understanding on my part, maybe a crutch for her habit. In any case, I knew it could never stand the test of time.

Now you are probably wondering, Doc, why I never mentioned my abuse while I was in Elliott. You see I was really happy there, about as happy as I have ever been. But the effects of the abuse have always been with me. For it was in Elliott that I first had the dream of being trapped in a room and Fr. Whiskers trying to hold me down as I reached out in vain for the window. Through the window you could see a piece of the moon It gave out a solitary light. But no matter how hard I tried to get to that light, I couldn't. Fr. Whiskers kept me pinned to the floor.

It was also in Elliott where my unexplained and sudden changes of mood struck once again. It was the same mood change that haunted me for my entire year in grade thirteen. Only that time I took out my anger and frustration on my mother. I ignored her for the better part of that year simply because I was so full of self pity and anger. For no reason at all, a dark, gloomy pall would overcome me and I would descend into that loneliest of worlds. It was during this time that I wished to avoid human contact. I tried to keep it to myself but occasionally it would spill over and affect someone else. I usually took it out on the dog and he, in typical fashion, gave up himself for me. It's like I said before. There is always someone lower on the pyramid who is forced to put up with your shit. This was a mood that would visit me often throughout my life and I hated it.

Cancer comes in many different forms, doesn't it Doc? I remember when my stepfather died. He was a smoker. I never really told you much about him. He and my mom married when I was fifteen. I think that was another reason I didn't talk much at home. I was used to being the man in the house and I suppose I resented him being there. But, in time, I did learn to love him. He used to smoke a pipe and used Old Chum pipe tobacco. I used to love the smell of that tobacco when I was a kid. But I remember when I first noticed that he was sick. He was a stubborn old guy, an old school type of person who would never be beholden to anyone. He was the proudest man I ever knew. He probably never went to see the doctor because he was too proud. That was Pop.

He was a world war one veteran who left home in Wales when he was thirteen. His first wife was an invalid and he took care of her in his own modest little home. He would never see her in a hospital. She couldn't walk so he carried her. He bathed her and looked after her every need. He was like that with anyone. He wanted to take care of those less fortunate than he but when it came to himself, he wanted nor accepted no help. He seldom went to church but he lived a life that would make a just God proud. He had a great sense of humour too. He did convert to Catholicism when he met my mom and confided in us later that at his first confession, he said to the priest, "put me down for everything but murder." He was a great man. Oh, he wasn't a world leader or world changer but I wouldn't be surprised if you looked up the word proud in the dictionary that you would find his picture.

Anyway, the first time I noticed he was sick, I saw him coughing up blood. He was on his way to work when this happened and he didn't see me looking at him. He just coughed into his handkerchief, put on his winter coat, lit his pipe and headed out into the cold to go to work. He knew he was dying but as he did throughout his own life, he bothered no one, not even my mom. He used to say "three score and ten," that's all we can ever expect. I learned so much from that man but I never realized it at the time. I was just a young punk who knew everything and was concerned, for the most part, only for myself.

Life for me seemed to be like being on a ship at sea during a storm. It has been a turbulent voyage. But when your ship is being tossed and turned, it's hard to see what's out there. There was a beautiful expanse in front of me but I couldn't see it. It's like those times when I turned my back on God. When I turned around, there She was, still in the same place She always was. In a way, my teenage years were like that.

But Pop died a terrible death. My, did he suffer with lung cancer that spread and ate away at him. It seems that people have to suffer darkness before being allowed into the light. One of my favourite writers, John Steinbeck, used to say that the only road to wisdom is through pain. Hell, I guess then you would think that I should be a lot wiser by now. First my father, then my stepfather, my mom, my young sweetheart, my brother-in-law, my sisters, and my first born son. I'll tell you about that later. I guess we need to know that death is part of living and maybe the easiest part for many. But whether it's cancer or a heart problem, it's waiting for us all.

But, as I was saying, there are many types of cancer and soon enough we will have to learn how to deal with whatever fate awaits us. But, to me, the worst type of cancer is the one that is inflicted on a child by a pedophile because it eats away at you and alters the course that God had in mind for you. It plays with God's plans. It breaks your compass. It causes turbulence and it seems you spend the rest of your life trying to right your ship and calm the waters. But miracles do happen and there are angels who help you along the way. The angel that saved me was my wife and this is her story.

Chapter Twenty Two

Did you ever meet anyone from the Maritimes you didn't like, Doc? I often hear people saying that. My wife is a Newfy, the very best kind of Maritimer. They say that the only thing a Newfy ever really needs is the company of others. They love to be in the company of others and before long, when they get together, someone will start on the guitar or the accordion or the piano. And do you know what their favourite topic of conversation is? Newfoundland. They love to talk about Newfoundland. They sing about it and they dance to its songs. And laugh? That's what I like most of all, their laughter. They're a proud province too and they're like brothers and sisters to one another. It's like the whole province is one big party loving family.

Once, when I was in Newfoundland, I picked up a St. John's newspaper. On one of the pages, I read the following headline: Mainlander Dies. I read the article and it was about a ninety year old woman who was born in Nova Scotia but moved to Newfoundland when she was one. She lived eighty nine of her ninety years in Newfoundland yet she was referred to as a mainlander. I guess you just have to be born there if you want to lay claim to their rich heritage.

I know I never met anyone from the Maritimes that I didn't like. Generally, they are people persons, interested in others, living for others. During the 9/11 tragedy, many planes were diverted to Gander, Newfoundland. The Newfies were ready for the more than five thousand stranded travellers. They opened their homes. In fact, in this town, their homes were never locked. They gave up their beds. They fed the passengers. They invited them to take their cars and tour the area. The stores supplied them with all the essentials, toothbrushes and toothpaste, soap, shampoo, you name it, and they never expected anything in return.

They were guests of this little town for over a week and after it was all over and two years had passed, one couple from Texas returned to that little town to thank once again the family that took them in. These well to do Americans offered the family an all expense paid holiday to anywhere they wanted to go, anywhere in the world. Where did they want to go? Seventy five miles away in the same province to visit friends that they hadn't seen for years.

Why do I tell you this story? Because that same little town whose life was endured by a collective heart beat was the same town where my wife was born. How lucky am I? Was God looking out for me or what? I don't know why She blessed me the way She did but I know I will never be able to express my thanks adequately.

Anyway, when I first saw my wife I fell in love with her, immediately. You don't believe me? Why are you smiling? What are you thinking? You don't believe in love at first sight? Well, I do because it happened to me. I met her at a dance and when I said hello and she answered back, I knew I had met the girl I was going to marry. I could feel it in my guts. I was completely and utterly smitten. More than anything I think it was her eyes. Oh, she was pretty anyway but her eyes. They were so alive, like there was a little light behind them, bright and alert. They say that the eyes are the mirror of the soul and if that is the case then I caught a glimpse of a soul that was pure and innocent, compassionate and full of love. I looked into her eyes and liked what I saw. But if there was any doubt at all about my attraction and instant love for her, when I heard her laughter, any possible doubt was erased. She laughed easily and without inhibition. Her laughter seemed to start at her toes and rumble up through her belly, and like a volcano erupting, out would come this beautiful laughter that only God could have made. I felt like Hercules on one of his voyages. He had been warned that when he passed by a certain island he would hear the sirens, voices of beautiful maidens on the shore beckoning to him and he would find them irresistible. So he tied himself to the mast so he could ward off their magical voices. I was not tied down and gave in instantly. I had met my match.

When I awoke the following day, my mom couldn't wait to ask me about my evening of the night before. I told her I had met the girl I was going to marry. True to form, she never questioned my judgment which was something I always loved about my mother. She led and taught by example and believed that if she did that and with the help of God, her children would be fine. She wanted to meet my future wife.

When I brought her into our home for the first time, my mother was sitting behind her sewing machine. I can still see her. She was also a Maritimer, a French Canadian Nova Scotia bluenoser. A beautiful woman with curly black hair, she had a needle in her mouth while she fiddled with the machine. It was one of those old fashioned sewing machines with a pedal. Looking up at my wife over her glasses, she smiled and immediately, as my wife told me later, a connection was made and a mutual love was born. It was more than a Maritime connection although that didn't hurt. That's the thing about women, isn't it? They have this natural bond. They don't even have to speak. They just have an intuition that lets them know that when they are together they are both on their home turf, feeling comfortable in one another's presence. I can't explain it. I just know there can be and often is an invisible bond between them, something magical.

Before long, my mom was at the piano, entertaining my wife to be. The thing is we were poor but we had a piano and my mom had a gift. She would listen once to a tune and she would play it on the piano. She was always quick to share this gift with others. Her music was the first gift she gave to my wife, although my wife tells me that I was really the first gift. Who am I to argue?

When I met my wife, I was floundering like a fish out of water. I was still working in the advertising world as a copywriter, writing those cute little jingles that make people think they need something they really don't. I remember one campaign I worked on. One of the buyers in our company told me that we had a warehouse full of typewriters that we had to move. So I devised a campaign, one that was designed to make parents feel obligated to buy a typewriter for their kids. "Help your children get better marks in school. Studies prove that..." The whole campaign was designed to make the parents feel guilty if they did not buy a typewriter. I told you before. I'm a Catholic, a real expert on guilt. I knew the right buttons to push.

Anyway, my life was unfulfilled in advertising. It might have been all right for some people but it wasn't me. It wasn't long before my wife sorted out my life as she continues to do to this day. Ours is a love story that has no end, very one sided and for this I have regret. In contrast with mine, her soul seemed to be always at peace. But her endless reservoir of love which she gave to me sustained me through some difficult times, even those times when that inevitable pall overtook me and inexplicably I would move away from her.

After our first year of marriage, our first child was stillborn. My wife carried that child, a boy, for nine months and then lost it. She did everything the doctors told her to do. She stayed off her feet and spent three weeks in the hospital prior to the loss. She was heart broken and so was I. It was difficult for both of us but more so for her. She was born to love and to give love. As a woman, she was God's partner in creation. Her very reason for being had been denied and she was devastated. I sat in a local park before going to see her in the hospital and I cried. I cried because my wife who only knew how to love had lost something precious. It was a bad joke that God played on her. He offered her a child and then took it away. I talked with God again.

"I don't know why you allowed this to happen. You, more than anyone, should know what a great mother she would be. You let misguided teenage girls get pregnant and have abortions or put their babies up for adoption. Then when you have someone like her, you stop her from doing what I know you really want her to do. I know, I know. You have a reason for everything you do. But this time, it's going to take a lot of convincing. Right now I don't like you very much but I would really like it if you would help me out here. I'm going in to see her now and I need you to please give me the right words to say to her. Help me to help her recover. Give me the right words."

I thought about this on my way into the hospital and when I saw her, I told her I loved her. I could see the sadness in those beautiful eyes and it broke my heart. I asked what she thought about the idea of my going back to school, to university. Immediately, without hesitation, she said it was a great idea. From the very beginning, my wife selflessly bolstered me. She made me feel good. We had saved some money, enough to get started on the first year of university.

We moved to the city of Windsor, across the river from Detroit, where I enrolled and where she took on a nursing job at the local hospital. She was making seventy dollars a week and we were paying seventy dollars a month for a modest apartment. We loved our university years and found that there were others just like us, young married couples, trying to get a start on life. We managed to save a little bit of money and every Saturday night we would go to the same restaurant to have our chicken dinner.

In our last year, she became pregnant again. Still affected by the loss of our first child, the next few months were nervous ones. However, the baby, a boy, was given to us just a month from the end of the school year. But there was a complication. The baby, healthy in every other respect, had a cephalhematoma. In laymen's terms, this meant that he had a huge bump on his head. It, basically, I suppose, was a huge bruise. They told us they had to operate as it had calcified which could lead to pressure on the brain. In any case, our happiness at having our first child was on hold. I talked with God again. I felt like Tevye in Fiddler on the Roof. Reflecting on the plight of the Jewish people, he once said, "Please God, I know that you have to test us by sending us troubles but just this once, can't you please test someone else?" Needless to say, God came through again as usual and now my son's life, along with another son and a daughter, is evolving the way that it should.

Fifteen years later, we were hosting a party and talking about the old university days. Very casually my wife asked if I recalled the first time I mentioned going to university to her. I said of course I did and that she was in the hospital at the time. Then she blew me away when she said, "I thought you meant part time." It never occurred to her that I meant I was actually going to quit my job and just go to school! A Newfy with an endless reservoir of love to give and I was the recipient. I didn't deserve her. I knew for certain that she deserved much better than me.

Chapter Twenty Three

Something terrible happened last week, Doc. My old friend Jack died. They said it was a car accident but I feel partly responsible for his death. He called me. He said he wanted to come to visit me. It was kind of a depressing visit to tell you the truth. I mean he told me about his condition, that he has a clinical depression you know. Anyway, he was really down and I don't even know why he came to see me when he was like that. I mean what do you think? Anyway, he told me that he never drank until four o'clock in the afternoon and then he would get into the scotch. I tried to get him to talk about his feelings about Fr. Whiskers and he told me that he hated the son of a bitch and wasn't sorry that he was dead. He said he felt betrayed, you know. I mean he had stayed friends with Fr. Whiskers over the years. I asked him point blank if he had ever been abused by him and he said no. But he did tell me about another priest who had him in a church basement once and asked him to expose himself. He said he wanted to see his dick. Well, Jack told him to fuck off and that was the end of it.

Now I don't know how much of this was true but I do know that four o'clock that day he asked if I had any scotch. I happened to have a bottle of it, not that I ever drank any. But my wife always wanted to have a bottle of scotch in our liquor cabinet because we had friends who enjoyed drinking it. So, I gave him a drink, about three fingers, straight up, with a little ice. I still had bad memories of scotch from the time I drank a whole bottle. I was so sick I thought I was going to die. I swore off the scotch after that and to this day I have never tasted a drop.

Anyway, Jack was reminiscing about our childhood, how we used to be like brothers. He told me about his teaching career and said that he lived in fear of one day having the R.C.M.P. come knocking on his door. When I asked why that was, he told me that he used a bit of physical force on some of his students in the past.

I could sort of understand that, you know. I mean it's not something a teacher would naturally do but sometimes you can find yourself in an unpleasant situation with teenagers and before long, you're in trouble. For the first two years of my teaching, I taught with a metre stick in my hand. Once in a while if a kid was not paying attention, I would slam the stick down on his desk and scare the hell out of him. I eventually stopped carrying the stick with me because I was afraid that eventually I might hit someone with it. It can happen. But for some reason, Jack feared that his past would catch up with him. After about four double scotches, Jack became very emotional and he started to cry. He told me what happened on his last day in the seminary.

Every morning, a priest or some other seminarian would knock on his door at five o'clock to wake him up. They would say "Laus tibi Christi," (praise to you O Christ) and he would answer "et cum spiritu tuo" (and with your spirit). He was then expected to wash, dress, and go to a common room for morning prayers. At this point, the priest in charge would tell them what was going on in the outside world. A celebration of the mass would follow after which the seminarians would proceed to the cafeteria for breakfast. Anyway, on his last day at the seminary, after five years of studying to be a priest, he was awakened by "Laus tibi Christi," to which he shouted, "Go to hell!" He eventually had a long session with the head priest and left the seminary the very next day.

He never told me why he left the seminary except to say that he didn't want to be a priest anymore. He said he hated himself and didn't know how his life had come to this. Doc, I didn't know what to do. I tried to commiserate with him but it seemed like he was in another world and was using me to vent his feelings. He started to nod off and I escorted him into the bedroom. I swear to God he was asleep before his head hit the pillow.

I called his wife and explained the situation to her. She completely understood and said that what happened was not uncommon. She also told me that Jack had a problem with his heart. In fact, he had a heart bypass three years previously. It's funny he never told me about that. In any case, she was just embarrassed that he got drunk at my place. I told her we would keep him overnight and she agreed. However, she said that he was liable to wake up suddenly and leave on his own. If he did that, I was to let her know.

My wife and I were talking about this strange visit and before we knew it, Jack appeared. He apologized for his demeanour and said that he was okay to drive home. I tried to talk him out of it but he had his mind made up. He left and I phoned his wife and told her what happened. She agreed to phone me when he arrived home. That was the last time I ever saw Jack, my childhood friend. I learned of his death on the eleven o'clock news.

He had fallen asleep in his car and ran into a telephone pole. I did go to his funeral and met the rest of his family, his kids and his grandkids. I talked with his wife and told her how sorry I was and that I felt responsible because I let him go and she told me that it was not my fault, that

Jack was like that, headstrong and no one would ever be able to tell him what to do. She also knew about my situation and why I contacted Jack in the first place. She told me that in her opinion, Jack had been abused like me but he never tried to deal with it. She also said that was the reason he didn't want to talk about religion with anyone. She was an amazing woman who had obviously endured much hardship in her life but had a calm about her that was so noticeable. I knew her to be a woman of great faith.

On the way home, I talked with Jack just the way I talk with God. I asked him what happened and prayed that he was okay. In my mind's eye, I saw him smile at me and tell me not to worry, that he was where he wanted to be now. Riding down that highway, alone, surrounded by darkness, I wept. I wept for all the unnecessary suffering and asked why She would allow this to happen. I know. I know. Free will, right? I couldn't help it. I was pissed off with Her again.

Anyway, Doc, I feel terrible about this. It makes me sick to think that a person's life can end like that without any kind of reconciliation. And, yes, I think I know what you're thinking. You're thinking that he deliberately ran into that pole aren't you? I believe you're right. Where does all this suffering end, Doc? Why am I still here? I think I'm ready to write that letter to Fr. Whiskers now.

Chapter Twenty Four

Dear Fr. Whiskers

It was suggested to me that I write a letter to you and even if I did not mail it, the act of putting my thoughts down on paper would be therapeutically beneficial. I recall offering the same advice to my own students over the years, the reason being the same. Express your thoughts, remove them from inside of you, externalize them, write to a captive audience so that you don't have to worry about body language and give them time to think about the letter's contents before you face them. This was an excellent strategy for me. For these reasons I am writing you.

When I was twelve years old, you violated me and the effects of that violation have tracked me throughout my entire life. Because of what you did, I have never been able to love unconditionally. My relationship with my wife, the best person I have ever met, has not been what it could have been. My relationship with my children could have been more natural. I have never been able to hug them in the way a normal father could do. I guess I didn't trust myself. My reluctance to trust others, especially males and especially priests, has been a constant throughout my lifetime.

I know now that I was very vulnerable as a young boy. I had no father. I loved sports. I yearned for male role models. I trusted you and the other adults at the school. And you took advantage of me in your own feeble attempt to satisfy your lustful desires. Was that it or were you simply enjoying the control you had over me, the power? Did it make you feel like God? I often wonder about your motivation. Why did you do that? Did someone do that to you?

You gave so much good time to us as young boys. You must have had some good in you for doing that. Or was this simply a means to an end for you, a way to weed out your prey? Predators in nature are like that. Big cats will search through a herd of elk and seek out the injured, the slowest, the most vulnerable. Is that what you were doing? Why? I know of two others you took advantage of also. One was my best friend Jack. Do you remember him? You know he's dead now too, don't you? Was that because of you? I can't believe how much anger I feel for you right now. And you probably don't even remember me. Are all of your conquests just a blur inside that confused brain of yours? What has happened to all the lives you violated? How have their loved ones been affected? How many lives have fallen short of realizing their potential because of you?

As a young man growing up, I was taught to love God and to trust in Him. I did this completely and She has blessed me countlessly in other ways. But when I encountered you, you diminished my faith, not in God, but in priests and in the Catholic church, two pillars I was taught to embrace unconditionally. My faith in God remains steadfast and I pray often that She will show me the way out of this inescapable tomb that your selfish actions have put me in. I want to love my family unconditionally and I want to trust others. I want to be able to hug spontaneously and I want to be able to receive hugs without freezing up inside.

We were always taught that we were made in the image and likeness of God. I do not see God in you. I see God in so many people, in their smiles, in their yearnings to help others, in their laughter and in their concern, compassion, understanding, sensitivity and empathy for others. I am disappointed that you, as a priest, have not shown this. Isn't that what a just and loving God would want us to be like?

Disappointment, frustration, and anger are some of the emotions I feel. Sometimes I think I would like to encounter you one on one and beat you physically. Sometimes the prospect of this actually excites me and at other times makes me feel full of shame, especially now that you're dead anyway. Who killed you anyway? Was it someone like me? Can you understand the rage of the person who did this to you? But these reactions, I consider to be normal because we are all human. You need to come to grips with your humanity and mine. We have much in common at least on the emotional level. It's these emotions that inhibit the full development of our spiritual natures. I thought you would know that. How can you return your immortal soul to a just and loving God if you don't first shed these human impediments? That's what I am trying to do. I have carried too much extra baggage around with me all my life. Now I am trying to unload. My psychiatrist is helping me do that.

How do I feel about you? I don't really know. I don't hate you right now but at times I admit that my hate was enormous. I suppose I feel sorry for you because you, like me, have never realized your full potential either. I do feel sorry that your life has come to such a tragic end. If you want to know the truth, I pray for both of us. Some day, a just and loving God will hopefully straighten this mess out.

I wonder if you even remember me. How many kids did you violate anyway? You were a good mentor and coach. Surely, you remember how you lured me into that puny little office opposite where we used to play floor hockey in the church basement. I thought you wanted to talk with me about sports. You knew how much I used to love playing any kind of sports. I didn't know you were going to wrestle with me, fondle me the way you did, rub against me with your body and your grizzly face. I didn't know you were going to lock me in your vice grip until you satisfied your lust. Surely, you remember me and remember what you did. I want you to remember and I need you to ask God for forgiveness. Mostly, I need you to tell me that what you did was horribly wrong and I need you to tell me that you are sorry. I need you to ask me for forgiveness. Please don't tell me that you don't remember me.

I never played sports as an older teenager. I told everyone that it was because I wanted to concentrate on my studies. I think you had something to do with that decision. Up to that time, I lived for sports, loved basketball, football and hockey. I was always the first person in the school in the morning, often arriving before seven o'clock just so I could get into the gym and throw hoops. I was often the last one to leave the school at night, staying late after practice, whether football or basketball. But in my final year, the weight of carrying around all that guilt and shame from what you did to me came crashing down on me.

I was miserable because I did not know how to deal with my feelings. Like many others who experienced the same, I began to drink and I hardly ever talked with anyone in my family and often thought of taking my own life by the time I was seventeen. I didn't know with whom I could talk. I thought my family would not believe me (now I realize they would have been my greatest supporters) and I could certainly not turn to a priest for guidance. What I did do is I talked with God all the time and asked Him to keep me alive long enough so I could understand and learn to live with my secret. It was God who pulled me through those years. And all the while you were there with other little boys. You never knew how I felt. You probably never gave it a thought. But I need to tell you now because I want you to know what you did and I want you to tell me that you are sorry.

There are so many reported cases of sexual abuse on young people by so called adults who find themselves in a position of authority. From what I have read and seen, I must say that what you did to me is small in comparison to what has happened to others. I know of the effects of your actions. I can only guess at the effects on others. This in no way mitigates what you have done. But it may account for my numbness or reluctance to be so angry with you or to seek revenge of some kind. Probably if you told me you were sorry and that you apologized to all of your victims and showed a genuine desire to reconcile with your God, I would feel so much better. As of yet, I don't really know what it would take.

Another point that really bothers me is my inability to think of myself as being on the same level as you or any other priest for that matter. I was always taught to respect priests and to regard them as God's representatives here on earth. I still have a certain respect for priests but definitely regard them as human. I have felt subjugated by your actions and I hate the feeling. I don't understand why I should feel lower than you when you are the one who violated me.

I also don't understand why my self esteem took such a beating over the years. I have been able to do many things with my life but I often think I could have done more. I think I was negatively reinforced by your actions. I suppose I felt used, disregarded and worthless. That's terrible for a young man to feel that way. The remnants of those initial feelings have lingered with me for a lifetime. Fortunately, I have a great wife, three terrific children and now grandchildren and we have been a good family. However, I am haunted by the fact that it could have been even better. For this, I believe you must take the responsibility.

I tried to contact you recently and really thought I was ready to see you and confront you. I was very angry at the time and did find that you were still alive, although elderly, and were dying of cancer. A mutual friend told me that your sins against young boys were well known and that your days of hurting were over. I even consulted with a lawyer as I struggled to find closure. Why have I not done this? I think, more than anything, my faith in a just God is the answer. I truly believe that She has a way of sorting all this out.

Finally, there were many years when I could never have forgiven you, many years when I felt hatred and disgust where you were concerned. Now, I want you to know that, as I near the end of my life, I am forgiving you. I don't know how you came to be the way you were, what chain of events in your life led you to be a child abuser. But, you know what, I don't really care any more. I have a loving family and a supportive family. I have received many fine blessings over the years and with the help of friends and family, I am happy with the peace I have. I hope, through God, that you may find peace in yours.

I stared at the letter, finally folded it and put it in my desk drawer. I knew I would never send it because he was dead. But even if he were alive, I couldn't stand the thought of seeing Fr. Whiskers, ever again.

Chapter Twenty Five

When we started these sessions, Doc, you said that I should think about talking with you about my earliest recollections, my school days, my teenage years, my relationship with my wife and about my career as a teacher. You said if I did that I would start to understand my problems and be better able to deal with them. You did say that I should feel free to explore any one of these topics if I felt they had any relevance. Well, now it's time to tell you some things about my teaching career, at least the relevant parts.

The very first interview I had as a prospective teacher was with a priest from Barrie. He invited me to join his school system as a first year teacher. I was flattered, that is until I asked him what the pay was. His answer that no one ever wants to believe was, "well, that depends on the Sunday collection," to which I replied, "Father what kind of speaker are you?" I thanked him for the offer but declined.

Teacher's college for me was a bit of a joke. Honestly, they didn't tell you how to cope with all the problems or any of the problems you were sure to face. No one counselled me on ways to deal with pregnant teenagers, kids who drank too much or smoked dope or who drove Vans in the sixties adorned with flowers and curtains and sold drugs in the school parking lot. No one told me how to deal with the aggressive teenager or the gangs. Not a word was said about how you should react when you stumbled upon a young Romeo and Juliet, locked in a sexual embrace under the stairs in the back hall of the school. I remember a Science teacher at one of my schools, when she was distracted by the moans and sighs of two adolescents right outside her window. Want to know what she did? She opened the window and dumped a bucket of cold water all over them.

These kids are creative though. Like the time I smelled dope in the hallway. It was coming out of a locker. I sniffed until I thought I had the right locker, opened it easily and found behind a hanging coat an opening that led in to a long abandoned room. There they were, stoking it up and having a ball. How do you corral all of that activity and all of that energy? How do you expect to pass on the wisdom of the ages, Shakespeare, Dickens, Steinbeck, Keats, Wordsworth? Does a kid high on crack or some other drug really care about that? What does the kid who has been kicked out of the house and has no place to stay that night care? Does he or she really care about the wisdom of the ages?

Now don't get me wrong, Doc, and don't jump to conclusions when I say something. I had some great students over the years. And I learned more from them about the human condition than they probably ever learned from me. But my point is the problems of the teenager are many and varied. And all I'm saying is that Teachers' College just didn't prepare me for it.

I remember I was told to be fair but firm and not to become friends with the teens. Well, part of that is correct, the part about the fairness and firmness. But how could I ever avoid becoming friends with these kids? Hell, I wanted to be their best friend. We had too much in common. I understood them. I had already travelled their road and I survived and they could too. And if it meant that I had to become friends with them in order for them to survive, then I was willing.

Actually, let me be honest with you. Don't you hate it when people say things like that? I mean to tell you the truth and let me be honest with you? I just said that because I hate it so much. Does that really mean that I haven't been honest with you before but I will now? People should be honest all the time. I find older people and children are honest all the time. That's another way we become like children as we age. Sometimes older people are too honest, brutally honest, so much so that they can say hurtful things. I don't think anyone has a right to hurt anyone else in thought, word or deed. My older sister lived to be well into her eighties but the older she got, the more brutally and unnecessarily honest she became. I mean one time she said something very nasty about one of my friends. This guy had an unsightly growth on his chin. It was not all that pleasant to look at, to tell you the truth. Anyway, my sister just blurted out, "why doesn't he get that thing removed from his face?" I told her it didn't bother me and obviously didn't bother him. "Well," she said, "it bothers me." Go figure. Kids and old people. Never try to figure them out. There's a lot to love but expect brutal honesty.

Anyway, as I was about to say before I rudely interrupted myself, the best lesson I ever had at teachers' college took place in a nearby pub. Why are you not surprised, Doc? We had to sit through a class in Psychology, believe it or not. It was held in an auditorium with about three hundred and fifty students. I went to the first class and never returned, deciding instead to use my time more constructively in other ways. I read the Psychology book and kept in touch with what was going on in the auditorium, wrote the exam along with the others and passed. But every day during the class I would wander over to a nearby pub, have a sandwich, enjoy a pint and read my Psychology book. One day, this old fellow ambled over to where I was sitting and asked if I minded if he sat down. His name was Sammy. He was smoking a pipe and appeared to be in his late sixties. He never told me anything about his own background but said he figured I was a student since not too many people in the pub that was right next to the college were reading Psychology books. Anyway, Sammy asked me what I was reading and I told him.

"Are you really studying to become a teacher?"

"Yes I am."

"Why aren't you in class?"

I told him the circumstances that I wasn't in class because it was too crowded and no one would miss me anyway.

"Why do you want to be a teacher?"

"Well, I don't know. I guess I like kids and I think I could do a good job."

"You don't seem to be starting out too well. You should be in class."

I explained to Sammy once again why I was in the pub. This time he seemed to buy my explanation.

"Kids are very complex, you know. Do you think you understand them?"

"Well, I was a kid myself. I'd like to think I could relate."

"What do you think is the most important part of being a teacher?"

"I guess knowing my subject and knowing my kids."

"What about loving them?"

"Huh?"

"Do you think you could love the kids?"

Now there was a question. How could I possibly answer that question? I didn't even know what love was. I guess I always thought that love and sex were sort of mixed up together. His question threw me.

"How do you do that Sammy?"

"You listen to them and you respond to them and you journey with them and you love them in the best sense of the word."

He took a long drag on his pipe. I didn't know what to say. I mean I never even knew the guy. I knew nothing about his background. What kind of a person that you would meet in a bar would come out with something like that? Everyone has a story. I bet his was a good one. Anyway, there you are, the best lesson I ever had came from an old guy I didn't even know in a bar. Go figure, words I will never forget and they became the cornerstone of my teaching career. Having said that, don't go thinking that I was the best teacher since Jesus Christ because I wasn't. Man, there were days, I can tell you, days when I wanted to stay in bed, days when I should have stayed in bed.

The week before school started I was in preparing my room and meeting with the other teachers. I had a Department Head of English who was gay. Now what do you think about that? Are you homophobic? Does the very mention of the word gay make you cringe or are you completely liberal minded about it? Have your views on the subject ever been tested? Well, until they have, I would appreciate it if you wouldn't react in such a negative way. I could tell by your body action that the word gay has a negative connotation for you. Oh, what the hell, go ahead, I can guess you already made up your mind and I guess I can't stop you from doing that. Anyway, anybody who knows anything knows that gays are not the same as pedophiles. So don't go thinking that this guy was just another one of those queers who wanted an easy score. I'm sorry, Doc. I don't mean to sound so angry. I just can't help it today. But you know what? In those days, if parents knew that their child was being taught by a homosexual, I don't think they would have been too happy. In fact, I know they wouldn't have been at all happy. They would have done what they could to have the guy removed from the classroom. So, I guess we have had some progress over the years. Depends on your point of view, doesn't it, Doc?

You want to know the truth, Doc? I said it again, didn't I? Oh, well. God has been very good to me over the years. Unbelievably good. This guy was just like Sammy, the one who gave me my most important pedagogical lesson. It was really weird though. Jack, my Department Head, said almost the same thing that Sammy did. He said he would do anything as a teacher to connect with the kids. He used to be an actor. He had some bit parts in movies and continued his love affair with the theatre by acting in and directing plays for amateur theatre groups. He had a great, booming voice. I bet you thought I was going to say he had an effeminate voice. You see how you can jump to conclusions? Anyway, he told me that the best way to reach the kids, and you had to do that before you could teach them anything, was to listen to them. Listen to their stories and then love them in the best sense of the word. There was that message again. It was a message that I liked and I wanted to follow Sammy and Jack's advice but it wasn't going to be easy. I didn't know why then but I do now. I still had that invisible shield, like an iron curtain that came down whenever anyone approached me and talked to me about sex or about love. And I still had that inevitable pall that encompassed me at times. That was the way I was ever since you know what happened. I had to get on with my life just the way that Gerry the painter did. I was going to try. I just had to keep going.

But you know when the principal called me into his office to discuss the upcoming year, he gave me advice that didn't quite reconcile with the previous message. I was to have a four year technical class of grade ten students. The four year stream was for kids who were not university bound. Many of them, if they were lucky, would start an apprenticeship program. It was an all boys' class and they were tough. It was nothing for one of them to pick a fight with another kid right in the classroom. At least, this is part of what I had heard about them before I had even met them. And I have to tell you I spent a few sleepless nights wondering how I would handle them. Mr. Rogers, my first high school principal, who never once said, "it's a beautiful day in the neighbourhood," gave me the following advice.

"I hired you because you are a big guy."

Honest to God, that's what he said. Doesn't that make you feel proud that you're a teacher? In fact, I am six feet two inches tall and I weigh over two hundred pounds. At least I was when I started teaching. As I age, like everyone else, I am slowly losing some height.

"And I want you to coach the football team and the basketball team. I understand you used to be a pretty good athlete."

"I love sports, sir."

I mean what a sap. First year teachers think they have to do everything. Another piece of good advice Jack, my department head, gave me was for the first two years, don't touch any audio visual equipment. Master the art of questioning and listening. He would not encourage too much extra curricular activity the first year. He knew what he was talking about.

"I've given you a tech class and I think you can handle it."

"Sir, what happens if a kid starts acting up? What advice can you give me?"

"I told you you're a big guy. Take him down to the boiler room and kick the shit out of him."

"I beg your pardon, sir?"

I couldn't believe what I had just heard. Mr. Rogers was strictly old school, not too far removed from Charles Dickens' Victorian days.

"Just make sure that you hit him where it won't leave a scar. And another thing, hit him so hard the first time that he won't even think of hitting you back."

You probably don't believe me, do you, Doc? Well, considering Mr. Rogers was at that time in his late fifties, that meant that he was likely teaching in the thirties. Times were different then. Anyway, how's that for advice? Do you blame me for being confused? I had two messages, one for aggressive behaviour and one for love. Fortunately, I opted for Sammy's and John's advice.

But to be on the safe side, I spent the whole weekend constructing a classroom constitution for my four year tech boys. In it I covered every possible behavioural problem and the consequence for each misdemeanour. It was a four page masterpiece that I couldn't wait to give to these kids. I knew this was the answer. I knew I was going to be an effective teacher with this gang of thugs.

When I started teaching, school boards would hire anyone with a pulse. At least that's the way it seemed. The one I went to first was no exception. Well, no, that's not exactly correct. I remember this guy who had an academic doctor's degree and his wife who was equally well educated. Both of them were turned down for a job. I don't really think it was because they were over qualified either. I think it was because they were black and there were few visible minorities back then. In fact, there were no black families where I lived. I remember when the very first kid came to our school who was black. Most people say they're not prejudiced but when put to the test, they often reveal a certain bias. But that's the way it was back then. I'll bet even you are prejudiced, Doc. I know I am. Not about blacks though. Don't you think everyone is prejudiced about something?

So there I was, in front of these four year tech boys for the first time, over thirty of them, some of them bigger than I. I held my classroom constitution firmly in my hand. In fact, if what I was holding was a wet dishcloth, it would have soaked the floor. I was white knuckling my first official talk with a class. You bet I was nervous. I felt their inquisitive stares. It was silent. I wanted to speak but I couldn't. They continued to stare. Could they smell blood? Then a weird thing happened. I started to laugh and I couldn't stop. I could see the confusion on their pubescent faces.

"What's so funny, sir?" said one young acne covered teen. "What are you laughing at?"

Finally, I stopped laughing and I told them that what I was holding in my hand was a list of rules for this class. I laughed again. I ripped up the constitution and threw it into the waste basket and told them that if they respected me, I would respect them. I said I just wanted to be a good teacher and hoped that they could help me to be a good teacher. I said let's just get along. Now, I don't know where that reaction came from but I think there was some guardian angel looking out for me on that day. It worked. Now I'm not saying that it was a perfect classroom because there were times that I had to feign anger just to get their attention. But at least it got me through the first day. I never took a kid to the boiler room, though.

Anyway, from day one, I loved teaching. Now when I look back on it, I know why. There was something deep inside of me that wanted to really be a positive influence on teenagers. I understand that now but I didn't then. Teaching kids probably saved my life, if you want to know the truth. And I never forgot Sammy's advice. Anyway, in my first year, I taught English, Latin and Business Practice. Yeah, Latin. Right about the time when it was starting to faze out in the schools. But I had a solid background in Latin from my altar boy days through high school and three years of university. I loved university Latin. Now you know I'm crazy, right? I was one of eight students in third year Latin. Funny how that happened, but I guess you should know about this too. After grade twelve, I had to select either Latin or French to take in grade thirteen. Since French was one of my best subjects and Latin one of my worst, I decided to take Latin. How's that for logic? But teaching Latin was fun. I already told you why I loved it so much. It never changed. You could always rely on it being the same day after day whether it was a declension of a noun or a conjugation of a verb. The thing about Latin too was that it really did help you in English. It is said that two thirds of our English language is derived from Latin although that may have changed since I studied it. The reason I say that is so many words and expressions are added to our vocabulary every day. In fact, I've heard it said that if you were to compile a dictionary, by the time you were finished, you would probably have enough to start another one. History changes words as do inventions and cultural interchanges. But Latin, it is always there. Veni, vidi, vici will always mean the same. I'm sure Holden would have loved Latin.

In any case, I always thought that anyone could teach a very bright student. The secret to that was to keep them engaged and challenged. Never let them become bored. So, more often than not, I would give them a choice of books to read in the English class, offer them bonuses for extra reading and writing assignments. I always wanted them to feel free to explore their imaginations but, at the same time, I demanded good writing and intelligent conversation. That's what teaching English is all about - reading, writing, debating and, in general, effective communication, teaching kids how to express their thoughts in an original way and having the confidence to do that. I always believed that if the subject of English were taught properly, the kid would get to know better who he or she was and would become confident and comfortable in their own skin.

But the students who really turned me on, to tell you the truth, were the troubled ones. And there were plenty of those. And again, I didn't really know at the time why I was drawn to the troubled teen. The mind is a complex organ, to be sure.

Chapter Twenty Six

You know what I think, Doc? There's too much criticism out there about teachers. Schools are microcosms of our society and people should remember that before they come down too heavily on teachers and education in general. For every misfit teacher, there are hundreds of outstanding ones, men and women who consistently go above and beyond what is expected of them to help a young person in need. But there's no doubt about it. Schools have bullies, those who prey on the weaknesses of others. They have druggies and sex offenders. In fact, schools exhibit as much perverse behaviour as society at large. But just as our society spends so much time and money dealing with 5% of the population, so too the school can sometimes be handcuffed by 5% of its population.

Being able to teach kids was a privilege. And I taught for the love of it. If you are considering being a teacher, don't ever do it for the money. If you don't love kids and love them in the very best sense of that word, you will burn out. You may burn out anyway but your chances increase enormously if you don't love the kids.

Throughout my teaching career, I battled with fits of depression. I had no control over these episodes. I just wished for them not to occur during my working days. For the most part, they happened when I was away from the classroom when I had time to relax and reflect on what I was doing and what was happening to me. Teenagers, at least the vast majority of them, were not concerned about my condition. They were just kids and I didn't blame them. They had their own demons to battle. But I tell you, Doc, there were days when I couldn't face them. That curtain of gloom would descend upon me and I all I wanted to do was retreat from the world. At times like that, I wanted to have no contact with anyone. My wife, unfortunately, bore the burden of these times and still I never explained to her why this was happening to me. In fact, I didn't really understand it myself. I may have made the connection between my younger days with Fr. Whiskers and the depression but something kept me from exploring that. Is that denial, Doc? Is it because it was too traumatic for me to think about? I don't know what it was but I can tell you one thing. Teaching helped me get through some of those days.

I mean I loved teaching. Especially, I loved reading great writers, and I loved to expose the kids to Shakespeare and Dickens and Harper Lee. That was one of my favourite novels, To Kill A Mockingbird. When Atticus Finch packs up his briefcase and leaves the court room after a gruelling trial that only he had a chance of winning, an old black gentleman in the loft says to Atticus' daughter, "Stand Jem. You're father's passin'." That is truly one of the greatest dramatic moments ever written. Naturally, I cried the first time I read that. It still gives me chills. If you haven't read that book, do yourself a favour and get it.

It was the sixties and kids were in to drugs. Hell, who wasn't in those days? If I wanted to inhale some Mary Jane, I just had to visit the boys' bathroom. Most of the time the air was blue. Kids used to tell me that it was easier to buy a joint than it was to buy a pencil in the school. Teens are already complicated enough. Because some mousey little jerk decided to get his name in the History books by shooting the President, the whole world was shaken at its roots. Fr. Whiskers changed my life but JFK's death changed our world forever. If my life was a pebble thrown into the water that had a rippling effect, JFK's assassination saw a mountain dumped into the ocean and it caused a tidal wave of change.

Kids, all of a sudden, all over the world, started to openly rebel. They started to question authority. I always thought that was a good part of the sixties. I mean that was healthy, to question your teachers, your parents, anyone who was in authority, even your priests. I mean I loved my mom but the rule of the day when I was a kid was "kids should be seen and not heard." I loved the idea that kids were now questioning authority. That gave them confidence. I loved the story about my childhood friend Jack when he told that priest to fuck off. Jack had confidence and he didn't mind questioning authority. I mean why should you believe someone just because they were older than you or because it was written in a book somewhere?

I don't even think you can trust the history books. Because as I already said, history is in the eye of the historian, subject to his whims. I mean wouldn't you love to interview someone like Napoleon? I'd ask him right away about the photograph you see of him all the time with his hand touching his chest. It makes him look dignified some say. Right. In those days, hygiene was probably a big issue. How do you know he wasn't just scratching himself or some bug was in their biting his flesh or maybe he just had indigestion from too much of that French wine, especially the red wine? I can't drink red wine because it gives me a rash and makes my face too hot.

And how about someone like Julius Caesar? I wonder if he ever exercised. I mean, apparently, according to the books, he wasn't in the best of shape. He was partially deaf and he used to convulse occasionally. They say when he was convulsing, he was really in another world conversing with the gods. Honest to God, some of the best writers of history are spin doctors. They would hit it big in the advertising business on Madison Avenue in New York City if they were alive today. Come to think of it, that's where they all are now. They're spewing out more fabricated nonsense from their offices on Madison. Just look at the crap on television. Anyway, there I go again, off on a rampage. Why do I do that? Anyway, Doc, where was I?

I really enjoyed being with these young people. One thing about these teens is that you always will get the truth out of them if you're a teacher. If you're a parent, that's a different matter. Kids love to talk to older people but not particularly their parents. Occasionally, though, you do run into the silent ones, the ones who have a serious problem they don't want anyone else to know about. That would be Ken.

Ken stuttered a lot. Maybe that's why he didn't want to talk. Anyway, I was just a young teacher and I wanted to help every one of them. Ken became one of my projects. I identify with Ken, not that I stutter or anything like that but because I had this feeling of inevitability I sense with you, Doc. Like, sooner or later, I've known that you were going to get to the bottom of my problems. I knew what they were but they had been buried for so long it was almost like a dog digging in the dirt for a bone. The dog knows it's there and it's just a matter of time before he unearths it. That's the way I feel with you, anyway, and, to tell you the truth I try not to think about it.

Anyway, back to Ken. He sat in the middle of my classroom and tried to be inconspicuous. He knew that in my class he was going to have to speak eventually. Some classes, like Math or Science, you could probably get away with not speaking. But English class? Never. It was all about communication. So, I ignored Ken for a few days and he was happy with that arrangement.

Initially, I would just say hi to him as he came into my class and have a nice day when he left. Then one day I made eye contact with him. You could see that he was uncomfortable with this. So I did it for a couple of days. Sort of like breaking in a bucking bronco, one step at a time. Then, when I would ask a question of the class, I would look directly at him and to his credit he would look right back at me. Maybe he was trying to tell me not to ask him a question. I could see that he was squirming a bit. So, I would look at him and then ask someone else in the class for an answer. I did this for a few days until he relaxed a little bit. At least, I thought he had relaxed. Then I started to walk toward his seat and ask questions and look at him. Again he squirmed. Again, I would ask someone else for a few days. Then, finally, when I thought he was ready for the direct approach, I stopped beside him at his desk and said, "what do you think, Ken?" Pretty clever teaching technique, don't you think, Doc? Right! He looked at me and then vomited all over the back of the girl right in front of him. I left him alone after that. I learned my lesson.

But then one day, I was driving out into the country after school and I saw Ken walking along the side of the road. I stopped and offered him a ride. He said he had missed the school bus and was walking home. I learned he lived five miles away from the school. I offered him a ride and we chatted for the next five minutes until I realized that he was not stuttering. When I asked him about that, he said he only stuttered in school. What pressure this

221

guy was under! I told him that any time he felt like talking just to come into my class after school and we would talk. I also promised never to put him on the spot again. You learn things from kids all the time. Don't worry. I'm not going to throw up on you, Doc. I'm a talker.

Along with my occasional fits of depression, I would have the same recurring dream. You know the one I already told you about. I was locked in that room and it was dark inside. Fr. Whiskers was putting his arm around me as I reached for the window and I couldn't get away. I could see a sliver of light through the window but I couldn't get away from his vice grip. All I could do was to reach out for the light. What was that all about, Doc?

It seems no one is immune from problems. And believe it or not, thinking about other people and their battles was a help to me. I used to think, when I was a kid, that doctors would never get sick, that priests had a personal and direct relationship with God and that teachers were always right. I knew this teacher who kept a bottle in his cupboard in one of the many school portables and every day after the students had left, he would have a wee nip, naturally for medicinal purposes. What made him drink anyway, especially in school? I mean couldn't he wait until he got home? What problem did he have in his life that caused this kind of behaviour? How about the two teachers, both married, who were seen in a compromising position in the Phys. Ed. Office? You never know who is teaching your kids.

Unfortunately, for the students in their care, some of their after school concerns were of greater importance than the care and education of the young teenagers they were paid to be with every day. Now don't get me wrong. Many were rushing home to pick up their own kids or taking care of a sick mother-in-law. Whatever. But one thing for sure is that for every bad teacher there are ten good ones, people who willingly go the extra mile to journey with the kids.

I continued to talk with God. I already told you I had this personal relationship with Her. There were days when I didn't feel like talking with Her, days when I saw kids in the school trying to deal with their problems. There were plenty of those. You should know that every kid, really, every kid, who was ever sent to the vice principal's office for causing a problem in class, acted up because of some deep personal problem he had. Teens are too young to have to deal with life's problems. I mean, they're already on a battleground with hormones exploding all over the place. In any case, one day, on the way home in my car, my mind began to wander to the events of the past day. I found it impossible to put the problems of the young renegades out of my mind. Suddenly out of the blue a reckless teenager, failing to stop at a stop sign, raced out in front of me, narrowly missing my eight year old car. Annoyed and frustrated at the day's events, I honked insistently and the young driver, steering his new Mustang through the busy traffic, acknowledged me with a sarcastic waving of his middle finger.

"God, don't you sometimes think when you created a teenager, you might have created a monster? Don't you think that creation got a little out of hand? I know you would never do this deliberately and I know we are to blame. But don't you think, just once or twice, you could just solve some of these problems down here for me."

For some reason, I began to think of Brian, a Geography teacher and a colleague. He was a former police officer who once remarked that after five years on the police force, he began to suspect everyone, forgetting that the majority of the population, probably 95%, were law abiding citizens. I needed to remind myself that 95% of the students were respectful and law abiding. They would complete their assignments, wear their school uniforms, attend their classes. No doubt, they still had problems because as I said, no one has immunity. Nevertheless, I concluded that opening a school in the morning was just like opening a city. We had twenty two hundred students every day to take care of, in loco parentis, as the Education Act reminded us. There are countless small villages all across North America with a population less than that.

Chapter Twenty Seven

My wife has been my most constant supporter my whole life. I've been lucky. She is really intelligent and if she had her time over in today's world would easily have been anything she wanted. I'm so proud of her. At the age of sixty two, she received her Bachelor of Arts degree from University. I bought her a school jacket that said Grandma on it. In her day, girls took a back seat in the majority of homes to the males in the family. So, the main professions that were open to them were nursing, teaching or secretarial work. My wife, however, is a born caregiver. So, it was suitable for her to choose nursing. You would love her, Doc.

She was a product of a medical family, and we often compared the professions of medicine and education. She would often remark on the dedication with which some of her colleagues approached their job. Some, like my wife, were born to be caregivers. They assisted the ill and the dying with a an empathetic compassion that comes naturally to too few people. Unfortunately, just as in teaching, there were those who were not so dedicated. Even the doctors were similar to teachers, some putting professional pride before common sense, especially the male doctors. Some were reluctant and unwilling to accept the advice of more learned and experienced colleagues. Obviously there were great doctors too, like the doctor who came to visit my wife and me in our modest apartment in Windsor before our first son was born. He entered the apartment, threw his coat down on the floor and just went about his business, doing what was required.

I took great pride in and enjoyment from my kids as well. One day, I arrived home, after a tough day in the classroom, to find my oldest who was now in high school throwing hoops with his friend in our driveway. The family dog, a beautiful collie, who had been resting on the porch and awaiting my arrival, bounded down to greet me. You already know how important dogs are to me. As I emerged from the car, my son tossed the ball to me. With a briefcase in one hand, I took careful aim and swished one. God, I loved to play basketball. It felt great to be home. I had a great relationship with my kids, even though something was always missing. For some reason, I was unable to show them too much affection. I stopped hugging them when they were small. Oh, I coached the two boys in hockey and loved every minute of it. I especially enjoyed having a parents' and sons' fun game and wrestling with my kids on the ice. I coached them in ball also and I coached my daughter when she was old enough to play ball. I really loved them but I knew I was holding back. I hope they can forgive me. I really want them to know how proud of them I am and how much I love them but I've never really told them that.

One time when my daughter received her first phone call from a boy, I was shocked. This squeaky little pubescent voice asked for her as I picked up the phone. I demanded to know who it was. He told me and then he asked who I was. I told him I was her big brother and if he ever phoned her again I would find him and beat him up. She talks and laughs about that today, although at the time, she failed to see any humour in it.

Anyway, one particular night we had friends over for a game of cards. It was a school night and I was tired. It occurred to me that occasionally a person will think of a certain thought which, of course, if uttered aloud in the company of others, would render him, at the least, doubtfully sane. This was one of those occasions. I recalled as a teenager, walking home from Yonge Street in Toronto to Mt. Pleasant Rd. I had just written a final examination and seeing an older person walking along the street in front of me, I determined that if I could put on a burst of speed and just beat that older person, who was considerably in front of me, to the next lamppost, that would mean that I successfully passed the examination. My present thought was akin to that. If I could only make that bridge contract, I would have a good evening and a good day tomorrow. Crazy, huh?

Mercifully, after an another hour of bridge, a couple of drinks and a snack, we said goodnight to our friends and headed for our bed. My wife approached me from behind and put her arms around my waist. The iron curtain came down and my whole body tightened. I don't know how else to describe it to you, Doc. She was just being loving and I was rejecting her and it wasn't just because I was tired or because I had a bad day. I never told her the reason for that reaction because I never really understood it at that time. It wasn't the first time I had rejected her overtures. I never liked to make love when it was initiated by her. I know now that she always thought there was something wrong with her. How awful was that?

"Are you sure you're okay? You did seem restless tonight."

"I'm sorry. Don't worry about it. I'm okay, really. It's just the job. I don't think I can ever get used to seeing kids upset about their problems. That's all."

"Do you feel like talking about it?"

"I really don't. You know what? I just want to go to sleep. I'm so tired."

We climbed into bed and she leaned over and kissed me. Before I knew it I was drifting off into a dreamland that bore a strange resemblance to the day's events. I've always dreamt a lot.

Anyway, that night I had a dream. I just remember parts of it. I wish I had written it all down because I know you like to hear about my dreams. I remember walking my dog, the collie. What a beautiful dog he was! He was tricolour and we called him Prince. The thing about Prince was he never barked. He only ever barked twice, once when my son thought there was no one home and he had just come from school and found all the doors locked. He was with a friend who was much smaller than he was. They found an unlocked window at the back of the house and my son boosted his friend up on his shoulders and the young kid tried to get through the window. But the thing was Prince started to bark and the kid retreated. I know because I was downstairs working and I couldn't believe it when I heard the dog bark.

The other time my son was walking the dog along the green belt in back of our house. A car pulled up to the curb and an older man got out and started walking toward my son. He said, "hey kid, c'mere!" in what must have sounded to the dog at least a somewhat threatening voice. The dog standing right beside my son started to bark and the guy turned around, got in his car and took off.

Anyway, my dream. I was in a sleazy part of town. Don't ask me how I got there or what I was doing there. All I know is I was walking Prince. Some kids were sneaking around a corner and I wondered where they were going. And some guy was following them. Then Prince started barking and ran in front of the kids and even brought them back. Then my dog scared away the guy and kept circling the kids and running around them until they were all in a tight group and I was running around trying to keep up with her. Then this transport truck came out of nowhere and the kids were screaming as it bore down on them and my dog was barking and then something wet smacked me on the face and I had to pee.

"Are you okay?"

It was my wife. I woke up and my dog was licking my face.

I have the strangest dreams sometimes, Doc. What do you think causes them anyway? I know everyone dreams but mine seem bizarre to me.

Ken Hills

Chapter Twenty Eight

Anyway, one of the teachers on our staff was strange, to say the least, especially when it came to his relationships with young boys. I always suspected him of pedophilia but was never quite sure but the signs were there. Somehow he was able to weasel his way in to the families of some his students. He was able to gain their trust and everyone thought he was just the greatest teacher. He took so much interest in their sons. That son of a bitch. So much did they like him that they trusted him with their sons for a weekend at his cottage. That's when the stories started.

By this time, everyone had heard about the scandals in the Catholic church, not just in Canada but in the United States as well. In fact the problem was universal. Some people attributed this to the fact that priests had to take a vow of celibacy. That's bullshit. Celibacy has nothing to do with it. There are many excellent priests within the church. But the thing is that you have to remember they're human, made of flesh and blood. They have desires. They're capable of sinning. They are not gods. But it is also important to remember that celibacy has nothing to do with pedophilia or homosexuality. Pedophilia is an incurable sickness found in priests, in accountants, in teachers, in lawyers, in engineers, in every profession and in every walk of life. The Catholic church may have a corner on the guilt market but they sure as hell don't have a corner on the pedophilia market.

Anyway, no one really said anything about this teacher to his face. But I saw him one day. I was at a local gym and after my workout, I saw the bastard in the shower with a twelve or thirteen year old kid. I knew he wasn't married. He was dabbling. I could tell. And it made me feel sick. So afterwards, I contacted the Director of Education for our school board and told him what I had seen and told him what I suspected. My suspicions were ignored and then guess what. Shortly after I retired from teaching, I read in the paper that this same paragon of virtue had been arrested for child molesting. But he cheated fate, that son of a bitch, as he died of cancer before being brought to justice. Now what he faces in his afterlife, if old Fr. Lord was right, was going to be a lot worse than what he faced here. You never know though because God is all about forgiveness although that's one case I would have to debate with Her.

You asked me why it took so long to come to grips with the abuse. I guess the short answer is that I was so involved with the lives of other young people in my professional life that it was never at the forefront of my mind. Also it was so much easier to suppress, to put it away from me, to bury it. I think the word transference is relevant here. You know all about that but I need to talk about it. You know I guess in a way I was using the kids too because I felt their suffering. In fact, at times, it was almost as if I shared their suffering. I guess you can say that by trying to help them I was trying to help myself. Pain and suffering come at us in so many different shapes and forms. Whether it is sexual abuse, physical or emotional abuse, the common denominator is abuse. So, in a sense, it is all related as far as I can see.

I was once asked to be part of an intervention. A close relative was in denial of his heavy drug use and an intervention was organized for him at a rehabilitation centre. There were about twelve of us involved and one by one around the circle we were asked to briefly express our love and concern for him. People were saying things like, "I love you but I am really concerned about you because..." When it came to my turn, I couldn't speak. I tried but nothing came out. I began to cry and then I began to sob. I was completely overwhelmed. It was as if I had become the centre of the intervention. Oh, the others didn't see it this way. No one else knew about my situation. But I had never felt so much anguish. I felt torn apart. By forcing my relative to look at himself and to come to grips with his problem, I felt like I was being forced to do the same. I guess that's what they call transference, isn't it Doc?

Ken Hills

Chapter Twenty Nine

I remember a job I had once in advertising and recalled a quick test in which I involved unknowing participants. The test was this. Because each morning as the workers filed into their cubicles to begin their day's advertising assault on the unsuspecting nation, routinely, people would say "good morning, how are you this morning?" without showing much interest in the reply. Sometimes I wanted to say, "well, do you have an hour? Please sit down with me and I will tell you how I am." So, instead of this rudeness, I devised my own unique response to their morning greeting. Once asked "how are you this morning?' I replied, "housing problem" to which they would say, "that's great. Have a nice day." Hello! Is anyone listening out there?

My wife is so loveable and outgoing. She is the best listener I've ever met. I really mean that. She loves to hug everyone. She has a child like innocence about her that has never been tarnished. What I mean is there is nothing contrived about her personality. Her reactions are honest and spontaneous and she is open to loving everybody. Full of compassion, she is the first to offer help. And her laughter! Well, that is just the icing on the cake. It starts in her belly and explodes at the slightest humourous provocation. But like most Catholics I know, she has a guilt problem. Maybe it's based on her not wanting to hurt another's feelings, I don't know. More probably it is based on her own upbringing in the Catholic tradition. Now, those of you who are not Catholics may think I'm being nasty with the Catholic church but you don't understand. I am a Catholic and will die a Catholic and that gives me the right to constructively criticize my church.

It's like giving a constructive criticism of someone in your family. Don't let outsiders do it but if you're in the family, it's okay. Like when I was a kid I used to fight with my sisters. But I loved them and would have done anything for them.

When I say the Catholic church gave us guilt complexes, I mean it. If you were a Catholic, you would know what I mean. Whatever it is with my wife though, it does not detract from her smile, her laughter and her generous and open spirit. She deserves better than me. I want to be like her. I've always wanted to be like her. I want to love freely and openly. I want to hug spontaneously. I want to trust implicitly. Instead, I am suspicious by nature. Are you noting this because I think I'm giving you a fair insight here, Doc? The one thing we do share in common is our Catholic guilt. It's funny how I keep coming back to that isn't it? I guess guilt is a way of controlling people and that's what the church has done to me over the years.

Anyway, my wife used to come up to me from behind and put her arms around my waist to hug me. Every time she did that it was like a steel curtain fell in my stomach as it would become hard and defensive. She always did that and I always reacted in the same way until finally I noticed that she stopped doing it and when I asked her why, she said because she knew I didn't like it. I wanted her to do it and I wanted to like it but she was right. The more I thought about it the more depressed I became. I couldn't sleep and I became very moody and started finding fault with everyone around me. I couldn't understand why others couldn't see what I was seeing that all people were phony and insincere and that no one really cared about what I had to say and no one really listened and they were only interested in their own lives.

I began to reject all overtures of genuine affection from my wife. Actually, I shouldn't say that. I began to realize that I had been rejecting her affections all through the years. If we were to make love, then I was the one who had to initiate it, not her. This wasn't a macho thing. I really believed it was because of what Fr. Whiskers did to a little boy so many years ago. The way he grabbed me from behind and held me in his vice gripping grasp, that son of a bitch. You expect me to feel sorry for him now that someone murdered him? Don't look at me that way, Doc. Are you thinking I did it? I didn't do it but there were times when I felt like doing it. That's why I rejected my wife all these years. And she never complained. She deserves someone better than me. What a life she's had! What a life she could have had! To her, lovemaking was just that, it wasn't sex. Sex to me became a dirty word. To me sex had nothing to do with love. It never did and probably never will. That son of a bitch. I'm still mixed up about it all.

I told my wife about my childhood experience when we were both fifty six years old. Imagine that! Forty four years after it happened and thirty five years after we had been married! You want to know why I waited so long? I have been trying to answer that question myself. It's almost as if I have been leading a secret life, another life, all these years, you know. I told you I never thought about it because it was buried so deep down inside of me. Probably what started me thinking about it again was my unhappiness with my relationship with my wife. You see, I really do believe that when two are married, they become one in more ways than one. Complete trust and faith in one another is essential. But how can you have faith in another when you lose faith in yourself? My wife deserved better and I wanted to be a better husband in every way possible. That's why I told her. I guess that was what started the crack in the concrete that my secret had been encased in for all these years. Now, two years after my retirement, I am telling you all about it. And you know, it's been an interesting process talking with you. I have felt many different emotions just as you told me I would. I have felt sadness for the loss of a normal teenage period, self pity, although that is probably one of the most counter productive of all the emotional reactions, anger, guilt and satisfaction at staring down the problem for the first time in my life.

Anger followed closely on the heels of self pity. In fact, I was so angry that I have to admit to you, Doc, that before Fr. Whiskers was murdered, I went to see him and was questioned by the police. I went to see him because I really wanted to give him a physical beating. I also contacted my lawyer and just about started proceedings against him.

Chapter Thirty

Doc, may I tell you about my most amazing student? To say that Owen came from a dysfunctional family is an inadequate way to describe his background. What can I say about a thirteen year old kid whose older brother by two years was a heavy drug user, whose mother was a heavy drug user, who went home after school only to find both of them stoned out of their minds with drugs scattered over the dining room table? Owen's dad was a truck driver. He was tragically killed in an accident while hauling a load across the country. He never seemed to be a presence in his son's life. So what chance did this young kid have in life? What were the odds of his escaping his teenage years alive, never mind graduating from high school? I met Owen through one of the guidance workers who talked about him at one of our weekly meetings. How shocked we all were to hear his story! But rather than stay in his own house and experiment with drugs along with his brother and his mother, for some inexplicable reason, Owen decided to leave home. And so he did.

The problem was he had nowhere to go, no one to turn to, no one to even talk to. All he took with him besides a bag with a few necessities was his bicycle. For the next three weeks, he lived in a storm tunnel that ran under a main road in the city. Imagine what this must have been like for a thirteen year old kid. What did he eat? How did he take care of himself? Imagine the repulsion he must have felt for the home he felt forced to leave? Where did he get the guts to do what he did? And every day, after sleeping in that storm tunnel, with his bicycle beside him, he would come to school. When he disclosed this to the guidance counsellor and she, in turn, to the rest of the counselling team, and to his teachers, an in school adoption project was begun. The first priority, after the social worker visited the home to verify his story, was to find him shelter. The second was to find him some clothing. They say it takes a community to raise a child. Before long, Owen had a new home. He had clothes but one thing he insisted on. He had to pay his own way. This was unbelievable. He was happy to do any kind of work but he wanted to have his own money. I don't blame you if you don't believe this story but I'm telling you the truth.

Owen had a pilot light deep inside of him that refused to be extinguished. No one would have blamed him if he just gave up but he was a fighter, the likes of whom I never ever witnessed in my thirty two years of teaching. Initially, he came to the attention of the guidance counsellor because his teachers were complaining that he was often late for class and when he did come, he seemed very tired. They were also concerned about his hygiene. I wonder why. He was failing all of his courses, not doing his homework and missing assignments. He needed help. By the end of his first year, he seemed to be coming around. He started to pass his subjects and seemed happier.

As I told you before, like is attracted to like. It reminds me of a dog who can sniff out a stranger in a room who loves dogs. One day, Owen came to see me in my classroom after school and the despair that he refused to let rule his life, like lava that had been dormant for so long, erupted and he was overwhelmed. He cried like a baby, asking aloud why this happened to him, what did he do to deserve such a life and that he felt like taking his own life. And when his emotions were spent and there was nothing left but pathetic gasps of inhalation, he looked up at me and asked if I wouldn't mind giving him a hug. At a time when teachers were discouraged from putting even a consoling hand on a student, at a time when society was hearing more and more about pedophilia, even though I had great difficulty in hugging my own kids, I gave him a hug. I told him how proud of him I was and what an amazing person I thought he was. I told him I wished I could be like him. I further told him that a lot of people at our school cared about him and wanted to help him in any way that they could. I tried to assure him that, for the next four years, he had a home here with us.

In the years that followed, just like cream coming to the top, Owen's abilities began to surface. His computer teacher couldn't believe how easily he took to the computer, with enthusiasm and with confidence. He even voluntarily helped other kids in the room. His Art teacher began to see flashes of brilliance in Owen. His drawings, while initially dark, took on appearances of hope. He received the highest marks in his class for both of these subjects. The counsellors continued to work with him and eventually he revealed what he wanted to do. He wanted to go to college and he wanted to study graphic design. To tell you the truth, he reminded me a little of my old friend, Gerry. History, as it always seems to do, repeats itself.

We wondered how a young boy, without any family support, could ever possibly do this. However, we also realized that when Owen made up his mind, whatever he wanted to do would become a reality. He rode his bicycle everywhere, all over the city, rain or shine, even in the winter time. And the people in the area of the school community took notice. Owen was everybody's son. When, in his final year, he finally graduated, his adopted family of social workers, guidance counsellor, vice principal and teachers were bursting with pride. Never had any one of us ever experienced the joy of teaching more than we did on that graduation night. Our pride and our enjoyment were increased even more when the principal announced that Owen was chosen as the most improved student in the school and was awarded a brand new computer in recognition. Further to this, it was announced that a scholarship of twenty five hundred dollars was awarded to Owen for the distinction of being the one student in the school who had the greatest influence on the school's community. He received a standing ovation when he went up to receive his reward.

Now eighteen years old, Owen was about to start on an even more difficult journey. There was no one who knew his story who would doubt that he would be successful. He was awarded a place in the college's residence, and all the while worked part time to supplement his scholarship. In fact, Owen had never been without a job. Today, he is a successful business man, running his own graphic design shop. He never forgot us and visited us often at the school.

I wouldn't blame you if you didn't believe the Owen story but it is true. But you might ask how could that happen? How could a twelve or a thirteen year old kid survive what he did? It would be like cleaning out a swamp that was full of alligators and surviving. Impossible! How could he possibly survive? The words of a very special lady echoed in my ear, "God works in mysterious ways. It's part of God's plan, a plan She has for each of us." I know that there are many who don't believe in God. That's too bad. They should look into it.

Throughout my teaching career, I worked with thousands of young people, some brilliant and some not so. But they all had something in common with me and everyone else I have ever met. They all struggled with a problem of some kind, not as bad as the problems that Owen endured and maybe not even like the one I struggled with for so many years but certainly they had conflict in their lives.

I had immersed myself in this world for thirty two years and ironically it saved me from having to deal with my own problem. But it was always there. And I am convinced now that it was what drove me to become a teacher, like finding like. Now, ironically, in my retirement years, I have finally learned to face my own demons.

Anyway, the high school kids, with all of their suffering, were very special to me, Doc. And yes, my religious upbringing had a lot to do with it also. Every morning, I would ask God to help me be the best I could be for that day and to make a difference. Every evening I thanked Her for the opportunity. Why do you laugh when I refer to God as Her? I told you before God is all things to all people. She's genderless and colourless. But we have to adapt Her to our needs. Women are, by nature, gentler, kinder, more empathetic than men could ever be. So stop laughing. Get used to it. And if you don't believe in God, I'm really sorry for you. It's worked for me.

Now, where was I? Oh yeah. My mother used to say, "God never closes a door without opening a window." I guess everyone's mother used to say things like that. As I already told you, my father died when I was five years old. I wrote a poem about him once. Actually I'm going to write it out for you. Maybe it will help you to understand me a little better. I wrote this years ago when I was up North working for the summer when I had that job at the mines. You know by now that I used to drink a lot, excessively, you might say. I guess you figured that one out by now. I was really trying to drown my sorrows. I guess I was trying to forget about my problem. I still remember Gerry and Jake and of course Dr. Mary but I never see them. I just hope they are having good lives. That's the thing about me. You wouldn't want to have me for a friend. I'm just too unreliable. I'm a pretty good listener but after you are out of my life, I will forget about you. I don't know why I'm like that. It's one of those things I don't like about myself.

Anyway, I was in a bar in Sudbury with a couple of friends and we were drinking quite a bit when this man came over to me and said that I reminded him of an old soldier buddy he met in England years ago. It just so happens that my dad was in WW1 and he was from England and served much of his time there before he came to Canada. Coincidence? Anyway, years later, I thought about that incident and this is what I wrote.

Pubtalk

in a bar in a Northern town,
where I bought beer for oldtimers,
I met a man who said I looked just like you,
father that I never knew;
said he knew you in England during the war,
no doubt memories of beer filled nights
with long ago war buddies flooded his wet brain;
he may have thought of a lost love,
so wistfully he looked,
but he spoke of you and
through his words, I heard echoes of your laughter
from a London pub amidst the chattering noise
of a dart board piano bar with brave young men

who hid their fear and consoling maidens
who hid their loneliness;
he remarked how you lit up the room with your smile
and shook the walls and shattered glasses with your
booming song
and how you, the saviour warrior,
could start a pulse beat with a tender touch;
suddenly,
the memory of a loving father's hand,
bathing his infant son,
flashed through my mind,
and I, in gratitude, bought the oldtimer another
and said,
"this one's on my dad."

Thanks. Maybe that will help you help me a little bit. I guess I wanted to show it to you, Doc, because I want you to know how important my dad was to me, even though I don't remember him. I guess it's my way of trying to keep him alive. Anyway, I've been writing for a long time now. I find it sort of therapeutic, you know. I'm glad you liked it. I still miss him, you know. I really wanted to have a dad when I was a kid, someone who could play catch with me or take me to a ball game. That's the first thing I'm going to ask Her when I get to Heaven. Where's my dad? Then mom will be there too and Pop and all my sisters and my cousins, my aunts and my uncles and, of course, my son. That's something to think about, you know.

Kids should never have to deal with death. When they are born, their navigational compass is pointing in the right direction. Then shit happens. Kids should never have to deal with anything other than growing up and what comes naturally. Don't you agree, Doc?

245

Chapter Thirty One

I didn't tell you, Doc, that I went to visit Fr. Whiskers not too long ago. He was in his eighties. Naturally, I didn't know what to expect. I hardly could think about why I wanted to see him. I just knew it was something I needed to do. I guess you would call it closure. I was nervous, my stomach was churning and the iron curtain was firmly in place. I didn't know what my reaction would be. God knows there were times when I thought if I ever met up with him again, I would kick the shit out of him.

One of the older priests showed me into the room. He was a kindly gentleman with a cherubic face and white curly hair. I noticed his black, shiny shoes. He spoke softly and pointed into the room. God knows I cursed Father Whiskers many times throughout my life. But then I saw him. He was sitting in a corner of the room by a window just staring. What was he looking at? His eyes were glazed over. He didn't seem to know where he was. Father Cherub informed him of my presence. He turned his gaze toward me and smiled.

Father Whiskers was a feeble old man who presumably could not even support himself as evidenced by the walker next to his chair. I asked him if he remembered me and what happened between us in that room off the gym. I told him my name. He squinted up at me and nodded his recognition. I asked him if he remembered what he did to me. All of a sudden he became restless. I asked him again. This time he shook his head negatively. I asked him if he remembered my friend Jack and did he remember that we used to play floor hockey in the church basement. Fr. Whiskers began to show some emotion. He was remembering. I continued to question him. I needed him to see me as a young boy. I needed him to apologize for what he did to me. He started to cry. The same priest who escorted me into the room earlier, the one with the cherubic face and the shiny, black shoes told me it was time for me to leave and that he would escort Fr. Whiskers back to his room. He asked me to please wait because he wanted to speak with me. I waited in the vestibule, not knowing what to expect.

The priest returned and came right to the point. He knew of Fr. Whisker's abominable behaviour as did others in that house. But this particular man was his confessor. It was public knowledge within the house that Fr. Whiskers had abused over eighty young boys. All he could do was apologize to me on his behalf. I didn't know what to say. I left feeling a mixture of emotions, anger at a second hand apology and no further recognition, pity for an old man and confusion about where this left me in my own personal development. It was something I had to deal with.

Because of my recent visit with Fr. Whiskers, the police did question me about the murder and were convinced that, although I might have had a motive, I was not their man. It could have been any one of those eighty boys. How many lives had been destroyed? How many compasses had been smashed!

I guess you heard that the murderer soon turned himself in. It was the same soft spoken priest who spoke with me that night, the father confessor, Father Cherub. It was bizarre really. Art imitating life imitating art. Remember that play I told you about where the nun shot a former student. She shot and killed him because she knew he was in the state of sanctifying grace and would go straight to God. Remember? And I told you how hard my wife and I both laughed at that scenario.

Father Cherub used the same logic when he fired a slug into the head of Fr. Whiskers.

Chapter Thirty Two

Now, I want to talk directly to you, the reader. Granny Munchkin allowed me to speak my mind. Granted, she was being paid well for her services, was not quite in the same class as Dr. Mary but was proving to be a very adequate substitute. I always required someone to listen to me and in that am no different than most. When I was a kid, I was told that going to weekly confession was therapeutic spiritually, emotionally and intellectually. And that, in fact, had been the case for me. But for such a long time and for reasons obvious, I was unable to take advantage of this free service. In any case, I was happy with Granny. Among other things, she assured me that it was okay to be me, that given what I had experienced as a young boy, my actions and my thoughts were normal, whatever the hell normal is. She understood my confusion and my hurt and reminded me that since my dad had died when I was five years old, that I was always on the lookout for a male role model.

Granny taught me that it was okay to be me and how lucky I was to have made such good friends over the years. She wasn't at all judgmental. Friends, she knew, were those who took an interest in you and would listen to you and be there for you when you needed them. That was Jake and Gerry and Dr. Mary, even though I paid her. They were my best friends long ago, and were there at a time in my life when I really needed them. It didn't matter who they were or where they were from or what they did for a living either. Our stories were intertwined. We loved and cared for one another.

But my very best friend, the one who has stuck with me over the years is, of course, my wife. Always compassionate, she supported me in any endeavour. She was and is my guardian angel on earth. Granny was there for me too although our relationship was a professional one. But she reminded me that there is a reason for anything that happens in life. She said that there was a relationship between my teaching and my early life, that I was an effective teacher because of my early life experiences. She reminded me how fortunate I was because I could have just as easily gone the other way. She couldn't quite understand why I didn't go the other way. I think I now know why I chose the road I did. I thought of Owen. Even though my troubles were far less than what he experienced, I could relate to his tenacity, his will to come out on top. And, of course, I will never forget Gerry and the painters.

My mother always said that our life is one long chain of events. Each event is linked to another. I never understood that at the time but now I do. In looking back, it is easy to see how one part of my life led into the next. But the fact is that now, in my older years, now that I have the luxury of looking back on my life, I can see what has happened and I understand how as the poet says, "I am a part of all that I have met."

Granny made me realize that it's okay to be angry and to feel cheated and to feel disgust and revulsion every time I read or hear about another abusive situation. She even offered insight into the cowardly, like Fr. Whiskers, those people who feel that they could only feel significant when they exercised control over someone else. It made them feel powerful, even though they were destructive. I saw them as more to be pitied than scorned, another cliche but a useful one at that. They were not lucky like me. They never had anyone who truly listened to them, to their frustrations and to their fears. Granny made me realize that life unfolds the way that it should and that no one in this world is immune from being hurt. There are so many in this world who are hurt more than I could ever imagine. But everyone has to deal with his or her own reality. Some, through divine intervention and good friends, can often turn a negative into a positive. To change my way of thinking after forty years of conditioning is a challenge, to say the least. But I continue to work on it.

By the way, I had that dream the other night, you know the one I told the Doc about. I was trapped in a room and couldn't get out even though I could see light through the window. Do you remember? Anyway, in my dream, the window was wide open. Oh, and one more thing. I almost forgot to tell you. I'm getting a new dog.

Epilogue

Child abuse is the worst form of cancer. It has a malignant and lasting effect on the victim. This effect is contagious as its consequences spread far beyond the victim. It eventually touches the lives of all with whom the victim comes in contact. It affects societies and countries. Eventually, it affects the world. In Canada, probably the most well known offenses took place at Mount Cashel in Newfoundland. More than three hundred former pupils eventually alleged physical and sexual abuse at the orphanage. Gordon A.Winter headed the Winter Commission which was charged with investigating the accusations. They issued a Report of the Archdiocesan Commission of Inquiry Into Sexual Abuse of Children in June, 1990. In 1992, four Christian Brothers, a Roman Catholic lay order, were charged with the sexual and physical abuse of boys at the orphanage during the 1970s. In 1996, six additional members of the order were charged with sexually and physically abusing seventeen boys at the same orphanage between 1950 and 1964. Nine lay brothers were eventually convicted. During 1996, the Province of Newfoundland paid $11.25 million to settle about 40 Mount Cashel claims.

The Police conducted an investigation in 1990 and laid 200 charges against thirty Christian Brothers. Counts ranged from assault causing bodily harm to indecent assault and sodomy. There would have been more charges except some of the Brothers had already died. Eventually, seven hundred former students came forward to allege abuse.

Lest you think that this problem is particular to Newfoundland, UNICEF reports that since 1956, over five thousand cases of child abuse by Catholic clergy have been reported worldwide. Thirty priests have been convicted of sexual abuse in France in recent years. Twenty one cases were recorded in the United Kingdom between 1995 and 1999, and thirteen cases in Germany between 1994 and 2001.

Abuse of children didn't just happen. During the 19th and early 20th century, the Canadian and U.S. governments attempted to assimilate their Native populations into the rest of society. The goal was to force Natives to disappear within the larger, predominantly white, Christian society. A key component of this policy was the residential school, which was operated in Canada for over a century, from 1879 to 1986. Most of these schools were operated by the Roman Catholic church and the Anglican Church of Canada. The United Church of Canada and the Presbyterian Church in Canada also ran some schools. About seven thousand survivors of these schools are currently suing the Federal Government and the religious organizations directly responsible for their inhumane treatment. The eventual number of plaintiffs will probably grow to over ten thousand. In addition to allegations of personal abuse, many of the claims are based on the children's separation from their family of origin, and the loss of their aboriginal culture.

Children worldwide are victims of violence as well. UNICEF and the World Health Organization, tell us that over the next twelve months, around thirty five hundred children under the age of fifteen will die as a result of physical assault and neglect in the world's richest nations. In Germany and the United Kingdom, two children die every week - three in France. More than one million children are trafficked across international borders every year. Over three hundred million children in the world work - some of them in hazardous conditions, some of them forced. Street children fight for survival daily on the streets of Europe and Central Asia, exploited by criminals, dodging the police. One out of every ten schoolchildren faces violence at school - some of it so traumatic that suicide seems the only way out.

These statistics are overwhelming but they don't tell the whole story. These kids, if they do survive, continue through life without a meaningful compass to guide them. The cancerous results of their abuse, be it physical or sexual, spread throughout the societies of the world. Is it any wonder we have wars? How do we stop it? How can we possibly reverse this seemingly irreversible tragedy?

Perhaps like Sammy, my drinking friend from my teacher college days and Jack, my first Department Head, Mother Teresa has the answer. When asked what we can do to help change the world, she said love. But start with your home. Love in your own home and the ripple which you start with that love will spread. And when it spreads, it will have the potential of causing a tidal wave of change.

Little children, I am with you only a little longer. I give you a new commandment, that you love one another. By this, everyone will know that you are my disciples, if you have love for one another. John 13.1

Reading Group Questions and Topics For Discussion

1. It is clear that the author identifies with Holden Caulfield. He even suggests that they are "practically brothers." Why do you think this is?

2. At one point in the novel, the author suggests that he has turned his back on God. Illustrate the validity of this statement.

3. The author also suggests that "it's really about survival, isn't it Doc?" What means does he use throughout the novel to survive?

4. Explain the relationship between the author's own childhood experience of abuse and his telling of the students whom he once taught. What is the relevance of including the stories of his students in this novel?

5. How would you characterize the writing style of this novel? Does it support the gravity of the main theme? By including humour and at times flippancy does the author in any way decrease the effectiveness of any message he wishes to suggest?

6. The author suggests at one point that he does not like bad endings. How is this feeling supported or not by the conclusion of this novel?

7. What is the purpose of including the Elliot Lake scenario in this novel?

8. What effect has the author's childhood experience of being abused had on his life? Consider relationships with others and personal issues.

9. Comment on the realism of the author continuing to worship in the same religion of the church that harboured his offender.

10. Must the church assume any responsibility for what happened to the author? Explain why you feel the way you do about this question.

11. Why did the author never tell any one of significance of his problem?

12. Explain how the metaphor of linking child abuse to a cancer is an effective one.

13. It is said that man is a product of his environment. How can this be applied to the author?

14. Very few names are used in this novel. The ones that are used are often make-believe names, names like Granny, Whiskers, Cherub. In fact, the author only once hints at his own name. When does he do that? What do you think is the reason for not assigning more names? Any name he does assign does not have a last name. Explain why you think he does this.

15. What dominant metaphors are used in the telling of this story?

16. It is obvious throughout the novel that the author is struggling to find answers to certain questions. What questions is he struggling with? What answers, if any, does he come up with?

17. Finally, how is the severity of this childhood trauma illustrated throughout the novel? What is there about the human composition that makes this lifelong conflict and the dealing with it a realistic one?

Other Books by Ken Hills

Ken writes children books. Each one teaches a special lesson. <u>Pizza Pete</u> teaches the meaning of love while <u>Billy Bluejay</u> involves the effects of bullying and what to do about it. Some children are painfully shy. <u>Milly Mockingbird</u> is about self esteem and how to discover your own voice. His latest book, <u>Henrietta Hummingbird</u>, soon to be released, illustrates how good things come in small packages.

<u>For children, ages 1 to 8</u>
Pizza Pete
Billy Bluejay
Milly Mockingbird

<u>For readers, ages 12 to 100 (or beyond)</u>
Sherwood Park, a novelette about two brothers growing up in Toronto in the 1940's

<u>For lovers of poetry and short stories</u>
Bridges

If you would like to write to Ken or find how you could order one of his other books, he may be reached at <u>klhills@rogers.com</u>. Ken's websites are <u>www.kenhills.ca</u> and <u>www.sherwoodparkbooks.ca</u>. Ken is a founding member of the Independent Authors and Illustrators of Canada. That website is <u>www.iaicanada.org</u>. Ken is also available for selected readings and speaking engagements.